Juliet stared at her grandm _____ _____ _____ ive
hope. 'You don't honestl^y th _____ _____ the
ship? Instead of going _____ choo. Do you?'

Juliet is desperate ___ prove to her father that a girl can be just
as good as a boy ___ ien it comes to business, but in 1794 a
woman's place is to ___are for her husband and home. The only
way Juliet can hope to convince her father is to change places
with her brother and sail on her father's ship on its next
voyage to Africa and America.

But Juliet's adventure turns into a nightmare when she
realizes the full horror of the trade her father is engaged in—
the slave trade, at its height in the late eighteenth century. As
she meets up with Dand, the Scottish crofter's son, abducted
and sold; Gbodi, stolen from her African village; and Hassan,
the son of a slave trader, Juliet begins to realize that her
greatest challenge is yet to come.

FRANCES MARY HENDRY was a teacher in Scotland for over twenty
years. She has also run a small guest house which only had visitors in
the summer, which meant she could write all winter. Until 1986, when
she won the S. A. C. Literary Award for her book *Quest for Kelpie*, the
only writing she had done was pantomimes for her local drama club—
something she still enjoys doing. She also won the S. A. C. Literary
Award for *Quest for a Maid* in 1988. Her first book for Oxford University
Press, *Chandra*, won the Writer's Guild Award and the Lancashire Book
Award.

Her other interests include history (until men started ___ ___ ___rs),
gardening, embroidery, and amateur dram. ___ ___ ___ ___es.

CHAINS

Also by Frances Mary Hendry

Chandra

CHAINS

Frances Mary Hendry

OXFORD
UNIVERSITY PRESS

OXFORD
UNIVERSITY PRESS

Great Clarendon Street, Oxford OX2 6DP

Oxford University Press is a department of the University of Oxford.
It furthers the University's objective of excellence in research, scholarship,
and education by publishing worldwide in

Oxford New York
Auckland Bangkok Buenos Aires
Cape Town Chennai Dar es Salaam Delhi Hong Kong Istanbul
Karachi Kolkata Kuala Lumpur Madrid Melbourne Mexico City Mumbai
Nairobi São Paulo Shanghai Taipei Tokyo Toronto

Oxford is a registered trade mark of Oxford University Press
in the UK and in certain other countries

British Library Cataloguing in Publication Data available

ISBN 0 19 275166 2

1 3 5 7 9 10 8 6 4 2

Typeset by AFS Image Setters Ltd, Glasgow

Printed in Great Britain by
Cox & Wyman Ltd, Reading, Berkshire

AUTHOR'S NOTE

Slavery was—and still is—common throughout the world. It may be based on race or nationality, colour or tribe, sex or age, religion, caste or class, politics or money, or any mixture of these, as ruthless or thoughtless people seek their own advantage, profit and power. People, it seems, can always find a way to justify forcing other people to obey and serve them.

It is not simply a black/white problem. Almost all peoples have enslaved their neighbours and rivals since the beginning of time. The Christian record is certainly horrifying. Whites, callow, ambitious, greedy and certain of their superiority, did enslave millions of blacks; they affected, often very badly, native people everywhere they traded or settled, and even wiped them out, deliberately or accidentally, as for instance in North and South America, Australia and Tasmania. But also whites have oppressed whites, as in the Clearances which made northern Scotland a near-desert, or the slave labour in German factories during the Second World War; blacks—for example the Zulu and Hutu—enslaved and wiped out other black tribes; and black and brown Muslims enslaved both blacks and whites across Mediterranean Europe and north Africa.

This book is set at the end of the eighteenth century, when humanist ideals were beginning to spread among ordinary people. 'Liberté, Egalité, Fraternité'; 'All men are created equal.' I have tried to show a few of the forms slavery took at that time, expressing the beliefs and opinions of the time in the words which people of the time would have used. Though my characters are imaginary, every fact or figure given here is, as far as I can check, correct; I should like to thank Professor Bridges of the University of Aberdeen for his assistance and advice.

I hope you enjoy reading the story as much as I enjoyed writing it.

Frances Mary Hendry

CONTENTS

THE SCATTERED LINKS

LINK ONE
Juliet, Hassan, Gbodi, Dand:
October and November 1794

Juliet: George's Dock, Liverpool.
The living-room of Mistress Sarah Smethwick.

'I've begged him to let me show what I can do, but . . . '
Flushing in remembered anger, Juliet imitated her
father's rasp. ' "The female brain is simply incapable
of business judgement, Juliet. Caring for her husband and
home, that is where a woman can best employ what
intelligence she may have!" '

'Buffleheaded slubberdegullion!' old Mrs Smethwick
snapped.

Juliet had to chuckle. 'I couldn't say so, grandmama!'

'If his ma can't, who can? Nincompoop!' The old lady
puffed angrily at her cigar.

'That's what he called poor Tony, just this morning. "Where
does the money come from, to feed and clothe you and your
mother and sisters, to keep you in every luxury? From trade.
My trade! You will not dare despise it! You will do your
duty to your family, sir, as I do! And that means, you
waste-thrift, namby-pamby nincompoop, that you will obey
me! Captain Owens will make a man of you, if anyone can!"
Poor Tony!'

'Will the lad go?' The old lady might be shrunken and
frail, too feeble to walk, even, but her faded blue eyes were
sharp.

'What else can he do? He can't stand up to papa's rages as
I can, he's too . . . nervous.'

The old lady snorted. 'Weak, ye mean.'

'Well.' Juliet shrugged. 'Now our older brothers are
dead, he has to learn to run the business, however much
he hates it.' Again her voice changed, to a whine. ' "A quiet,

3

respectable country parsonage, with my viola, and cricket, and natural philosophy—that's all I want! All I ever wanted! My final year at Oxford! And now, as if being chained to a desk slaving in the office for ten hours a day isn't bad enough, now I'm being sent on a voyage to learn about ships and the Africa trade. I can't do it, Juliet! Curse Richard's carelessness! And Sebastian's patriotism! I've to become a money-grubbing merchant!"'

Too upset to sit still, Juliet stood up beside her grandmother's wheeled chair, to stare out of the window at the bustle of the dock below. No wonder grandmama refused to leave her home, built in the loft of the warehouse where she had helped build up the business; she would prefer to live here herself. Broad Street, where papa had built his grand new mansion, was never so interesting.

Old Mrs Smethwick snorted in contempt. 'Cock-nosed flummery! It's that ma o' yourn, her an' her "my cousin the earl"! I told yer dad she were too high in the instep, but he told me he wanted to rise in the world! Marryin' above himself!' She puffed her cigar. 'An' see what he's got! That family she's so proud o', wasters every one o' them, aye sneerin' at him as if they're doin' him a favour lettin' him pay off their debts. Yer brothers were gawmless. Tony's right about that—there's aye a first time.'

'Mama boasts about Seb's patriotic heroism.' Juliet's voice was dry.

'Nowt patriotic nor heroic as I can see about bein' shot from behind a haystack be Irish bog-trotters.' Mrs Smethwick sniffed, as drily. 'Too full o' himself to see owt else! All yer ma's snobby notions, flashy red uniform, meet the gentry, eh? Oh, aye. An' then Dickie. Ye need yer wits about ye on the docks! Nobbut a fool walks under a net full o' kegs, in case it breaks.' Her face was bitter. 'No loss, neither o' them. Cloth-headed dollops, all me men.'

'And Tony worst of all.' Juliet flumped down again and beat her fists angrily on her knees. 'Oh, drat him! He has everything I want—'

'An' despises it.' Old Mrs Smethwick nodded. 'Head empty an' noisy as a drum.'

'He'll ruin the firm, grandmama! I know he will! He's useless! He can't think ahead, or organize, or even add up a line of figures correctly, let alone work out costs and percentage profits, or know what will sell in Rio or Cairo or Oslo or Bombay. He doesn't even know where half the places are. "What do I care about Murbles and Smethwick or their eleven ships and forty-three factors?" he says, and such a sneer in his voice . . . Oh, I could do so well! I could . . . But I have to go off to finishing school.' She mimicked her mother's high, die-away tones. ' "Your accent, Juliet! Deplorably provincial! And you do not glide, you stride like a man! Appalling!" Drat her!' Her own rather gruff voice was bitter. 'I'm turbulent and argumentative, I insist on thinking for myself, I shock and disgust everyone—like last week.'

Her grandmother cackled. 'Swore at a carter, didn't ye? Doxy!'

'Well, when his horse fell on the ice I told him it would be more sensible to find a sack to give it a footing to rise, rather than standing whipping the poor beast. He swore at me, so I swore back. After visiting you, dear, sweet old lady that you are—' They exchanged wicked grins, suddenly looking very alike. '—it just flowed! I flayed him!' She chuckled proudly, and then sobered. 'But mama's nastiest friend came by, going to the lending library, and she told mama, and mama had the vapours. So—school. The Misses Lazenby's Genteel Seminary for Young Ladies, in Bath.'

'Been talkin' about it for long enough, ain't she?'

'Yes. But now she's acting. "Beauty, I fear, is beyond you, Juliet. But even the roughest stone can have its jagged edges smoothed." Flattering, eh?' Juliet sighed. 'Elocution and conversation, etiquette and deportment. Charm. Vital skills like painting fans. Four hours' harp practice every day. All the sickening arts of snaring a husband.' She mimed spitting, enjoying her grandmother's chuckle. 'The other girls will be petite and elegant and proper and pretty and accomplished and . . . and London! They'll sneer at me. Oh, lud, grandmama, it will be stifling, miserable, sheer slavery! And all useless—as if any gentleman of mama's "proper social standing" would dream of marrying into a family in trade, however rich papa is or however many of mama's second cousins are earls. Oh, I wish I could escape!' Defeated, she sank back to her chair. 'I wish I could just take Tony's place.'

Her grandmother's eyes blinked like an ancient lizard. 'Why not?'

'What?' Juliet sat up. 'Oh, it would be wonderful!'

'So why don't ye? Go on this voyage instead o' him?'

'In a ship full of men? I'd have to dress as a boy for months. Don't be silly!'

'Don't come the little madam wi' me, ye uppity long-shanks!' The old lady wagged her cigar at the girl's dismissive tone. 'I'd not take that voice from the king himself!'

Juliet puffed. 'I'm sorry, grandmama. But—no. No. I'd love to, but I couldn't!'

'Why not? Wouldn't be the first time ye've acted the lad, eh?' Juliet's jaw dropped, and she blushed at the old lady's knowing cackle. 'Think because I never get out I don't hear about nowt? Two summers ye've worn Tony's clothes for a spree! Ye've looked in yer mirror, lass! Ye're the image o' yer brother.'

It was true. Although three years younger, Juliet was as tall as Tony; fantastically so, her mother mourned. He was slightly plumper. Their faces were almost identical, though Tony's mouth was sulky, less determined. Their wide eyes were the same slate grey, their hair was equally fair and naturally straight, though hot irons tortured Juliet's into ringlets. Both had their father's big hooked nose which made Juliet's life a misery among her prettier young sisters and friends.

Now she stared at her grandmother in alarm, astonishment,

a tentative hope. 'You don't honestly think I could take his place? On the ship? Instead of going to school? Do you?'

The old woman nodded. 'There's a many women have played the man. Workin' beside their men, miners an' such, or goin' as sailors to be wi' their husbands or lovers, or just escapin', seekin' freedom. Me own cousin Emma couldn't stomach the husband her dad picked for her, so she ran away, joined the Austrian army. Died in a duel in France twenty year back.'

'I never knew that!' Juliet was enthralled.

'Ain't talked about. Scandalous! Shockin'! But happens more often than ye'd think.' Her eyes were bright in their net of wrinkles. 'Could you do it?'

'Yes, but . . . I could, I'm sure . . . I'd give my soul to try, but . . . ' Regretfully, Juliet shook her head. 'You know what papa's like if he's crossed. I'd never ever get the chance to help in the firm. It would be wonderful, but no. I'd lose too much, even if I succeeded, grandmama. It wouldn't be worth it.'

'Huh.' Her grandmother nodded. 'Glad ye've sense enough to see it. But now I'll add a bit weight to it. Tell ye summat else ye never knew. Murbles an' Smethwick, aye? Well, I'm Murbles.'

'You? You own shares in the firm?'

'Who d'ye think it were started the firm? Me dad, Harry Murbles, shippin' wine from Bordeaux. An' when he prospered an' bought another ship, he hired Dick Smethwick to captain her, strong an' clever an' oh, such a smile! So I married Dick, an' me dad made him his partner. Murbles an' Smethwick, all legal. An' I had a baby—your dad—an' three more as died. But I worked along o' me dad, in the office, same as before, till we had five ships. An' then Dick's ship went down.' She shook her head in ancient, long-dry regret. 'Aye, aye. So when your dad was twenty-one he became a full partner, wi' his dad's shares. But when my dad died, he left his shares to me. Not to yer dad. An' as a widow, I can own 'em meself, I've no husband to take 'em over.' She nodded in satisfaction at the awe on Juliet's face. 'Aye. I own sixty per cent. Me. I've aye let yer dad run it. He's not a man to take kindly to his ma tellin' him what to do. He's forgotten now how much I done. If he ever knew. An' in truth, I grew tired. An' he does well by the firm.'

She lifted a hand to draw even more of Juliet's already intense attention. 'But now, you listen here, me lass. I judge ye're twice the man yer daft brother is. So prove me right. Show me what ye can do. You persuade Tony to change places wi' ye. You make the arrangements—you, not me. You go the round trip to Africa an' Charleston wi' Captain Owens, an' never get found out, an' come back wi' a good report. You do that, an' when I die—an' it'll not be that long now—ye'll get my shares. An' then yer dad can't keep ye out.' She sat back, panting with the effort of talking so urgently. 'It's yer single chance, lass. Will ye dare fight for what ye want? Will ye?'

Dress as a man, for maybe a year, on a ship full of men, risking discovery and social ruin all the time, on a slaving voyage, into danger and dirt and unknown horrors? What well-brought-up girl could consider it for an instant without fainting?

Open-mouthed, Juliet gasped, 'Yes! Oh, lud, yes, grandmama!'

Hassan: Djenne, Niger River; present-day Mali. The home of Farouk al-Jiddah, merchant.

The tall, thin boy burst out into the colonnaded roof garden of the women's quarters of the finest house in Djenne.

'Hassan! What is your hurry?' old Taranah, grandfather's wife, tyrant of the family, scolded him. Around her chair her sons' wives and slaves were resting from the afternoon heat on carpets and cushions, their cottons and silks bright in the shade of the arches and the green awnings, while their clan of children swarmed and played among them. A girl playing a guzla broke off in the middle of a love song. The old lady poked her stick at the slave girl fanning her, who had paused to wipe sweat from her face. 'Wake up, Asura! And you, Laila!' Alarmed, the girl swayed the big palm-leaf fan, while Laila plucked her strings again. Taranah's mood depended on her few teeth; if they ached, it took very little to anger her.

Now Taranah lay back, studying the boy, her husband's grandson. 'Heh! What is so urgent? You are usually very dignified, stiff like a secretary bird. Is the Dey of Algiers at the gate with an army, and you made general?' Hassan blinked, baffled. Taranah chuckled maliciously. *Ya Allah*, the boy had no sense of humour!

Bowing respectfully, Hassan glanced to where his father's mother smiled from the far side of the court. She was cracking peach stones to flavour arrack. Though of course wine was forbidden to True Believers, Haji Farouk, Taranah's eldest son, the master of the house, declared to the amusement of his wives that since brandy was distilled that was allowable.

'I was looking for grandmother, lady.'

'Why?'

'I can now recite the whole of the Koran without a single mistake or prompt! So now father says I may go with him on his next trip!'

'So! How old are you—fourteen? Well done! Farouk will be pleased, and your father proud of you!' The old woman led a gentle applause for the boy's accomplishment. All the women laid aside sewing or chess, baby or parrot or monkey; any break in the monotony was good for hours of chat. 'You wish to be a man of letters, don't you? Good, good—it is time we had a scholar in the house again. Djenne was a great centre of learning in the old days, almost as great as Timbuktu. But certainly some experience of the world and its ways is useful. So when are you going?'

'Soon, lady. Father has always wanted to explore to the east, far past Timbuktu, right along the Great River. Men say it comes to the ocean, where we could trade with the white men. And now Farouk has agreed.'

Taranah shook her head doubtfully. 'Uzum is always thinking of new things. Some go west for gold, but east . . . We go south to buy slaves, and trade them north to Timbuktu or on to the desert salt mines, or even right across the sands to Algiers. He could trade with white men there, if he is so keen. Away along the great water through the lands of the pagans? *Ya Allah* . . . Going to new places is a risk.'

'But also a source of new wealth, *inshallah*. It will be a profitable venture, I'm sure—and an adventure for the boy,' Farouk's wife dared to disagree. Everyone waited to see if she would get away with it, or be scolded for impertinence.

'Y-yes . . . certainly, if Allah wills.' Taranah finally nodded reluctantly. Anything new was disturbing. But she tried to be fair. 'Uzum has done very well for us in the past. And for himself, of course. *Ya Allah*, he must be as wealthy as Farouk!'

They all laughed again. Though his mother had been a slave, as a respected servant to his half-brother Uzum was allowed to keep a share of the profits from his work. Even so, to suggest that he might be as rich as Farouk, who had four brothers and a dozen cousins and half-brothers working for him, and had even been rich enough to make pilgrimage to Mecca five years ago—well, it was comical.

Dismissed, Hassan picked his way neat-footed past the scented pool, refilled by the house slaves every morning, that cooled the air and provided water for the big rose pots. Smiling to him, his grandmother called a boy to remove the baskets of shells and kernels and bring her water to wash the stickiness from her hands, and settled beside Hassan on her worn rug with a grunt of pleasure. She sighed to lose the boy, the only son of her youngest son Uzum, eagerly setting off to see the world. But she had a dream . . . 'Hassan,' she murmured, 'do something for me.'

'If I can, grandmother.'

Bakti smiled at Hassan's wary tone. Her grandson always liked to know where he was putting his feet. 'If you see a white man, ask if he knows England. That was my country, you know? I am from Turo or Cornal, I think, but I forget, I was only eight when corsairs raided my village and captured me.' He nodded; she had often spoken of it. On a trip north with slaves for the big markets in Algiers, Taranah's husband had bought the child, attracted by her yellow hair. She always stayed in shadow, for even now her skin, white like a plucked chicken, burned easily in the harsh sunlight. Her children were darker, and luckily Hassan was as brown as his grandfather.

'My name—I've almost forgotten it—my name is—was—Bridie. Bridie Treworthy.' She smiled again, ruefully. 'Certainly I have been happy here, some of the time, and what more can anyone hope for? And I never complain, what would be the use? But my heart longs for my home.'

Hassan shrugged. That was what happened to slaves.

'Turo or Cornal, England. Bridie Treworthy. You'll remember?'

'They may not know England, grandmother.'

She sighed. 'Maybe not. But you'll ask? My eyes weary for . . . for green . . . '

Green? Hassan glanced up at the awnings. They were as green as anything he had ever seen.

Gbodi: the village of Loko, near the modern Mali-Niger border. The hut of Monifa, third wife of the village blacksmith.

Gbodi chewed at her horn spoon, seeking any hint of flavour left on it. 'I'm empty as the message drum!' She scratched absently and brushed at the clustering flies round her eyes.

Her mother sighed. 'We're all hungry just now. But when the rains come . . . '

The sores round Gbodi's mouth and over her swollen stomach and her stick-like arms and legs would heal as usual

11

then, when there was plenty of food again, and palm oil to make her skin smooth and shiny. 'Will they come?'

'Of course they will!' Monifa reassured her fiercely. Her voice was deep and furry, normally warm and reassuring; today, though, it grated in Gbodi's mind as her mother hefted the toddler on her hip and turned to stare again down the village, twisting fretfully at the thong of her bead amulet.

Gbodi gave her spoon a final regretful lick and hung it neatly away on its peg on the mud wall. Even if she had had food, she could scarcely have eaten for fear.

Instead of pounding the last mealies or husks of millet, scouring the cracked, baked countryside for any overlooked groundnuts, fetching water or wood, spinning cotton, cooking, playing with the babies, any normal task, all the women of the village were skulking about, offering flowers and scarce scraps of food to their fetish snakes and house gods, anxiously rearranging the white stones that marked their ancestors' graves between their huts in case any of the patterns had been displaced by a careless foot. The children, the squabbling, laughing friends who played or herded the goats with Gbodi, telling jokes and singing, were hidden away silent inside the huts.

A woman was wailing. 'Is that Fola crying?'

'Yes. And no wonder.'

No wonder indeed. Four months before, she had had her first baby; but it was twins.

'What are the men doing in the juju hut?'

Monifa shrugged. 'Should a woman know? The doctor is trying to discover which baby is the god child.' She shuddered. 'See what happens when we have a god in the village! The rains do not come—after locusts and army ants last year, too! Abebi is dying. That will be four people dead of hunger. Only old ones, but . . . '

'The headman should not have let the babies live, should he?' For comfort Gbodi clutched at her bead charm, her only clothing. 'The juju doctor told him they must die.'

'Yes, but Fola begged him. She says her tribe prays for twins, thinks they bring luck, not disaster.' Monifa shook her head. 'Maybe. But here it is different. The headman is a fool about that girl, ever since he bought her from the traders two years ago. So we all suffer. So now we must kill the babies, and Fola must be punished, too.'

'How?' Gbodi asked, her eyes huge and round with worry. In her twelve rains, she could not recall any twins being born.

Her mother was grim. 'We will all beat her and beat her. Till she knows that the juju man knows the ways of our gods better than she does.'

'Will she die?'

'Should we care?' Monifa shrugged, grey with fear. 'She must pay for what her foolishness has brought on us. We must kill the god baby, and then sacrifice the other baby to it, to make it know that we fear it. The juju doctor says this is a very powerful, angry god. If we anger it, the rains will never come again!' It could kill the goats, dry up the well, attract snakes into the gardens, draw kidnappers to the remote village to steal children away, bring deadly sickness—anything! 'Remember your grandfather. He offended his tools, forgot to give them the proper tribute of a dog every four or five days, so his hammer smashed in his hand and sent splinters into his eyes so that he died.'

Gbodi nodded vigorously. If this baby was a stronger god, no sacrifice that kept it happy was too much. She felt bad, though. 'I like Fola.'

Her mother snorted disgust. 'So did I. What does that matter? Listen!'

Music of horns and many drums started. From the juju hut the Ejunjun came dancing, the spirits of the ancestors called to aid their children, filling the five young men who wore the heavy, worn robes and masks, whirling and kicking and leaping across the dancing ground. It was death to see any part of the skin of the men under the tall masks and bright, tent-like costumes of quilted cloth and straw.

13

Among them danced the juju doctor, spinning, swaying and stamping, protecting the village with his power, chasing away evil gods from every hut with the feathers and rattles of bone and teeth and tiny skulls dangling from his magic staff. On top of the ritual scars his skinny body and arms were painted in stripes and spots of yellow and black. His skirt of monkey tails and his leopard-skin cloak were old, but less ancient than the wooden mask which covered his whole head in a mass of carvings, a two-faced god with four ibex horns.

Gbodi shrank back into the shadow of the hut. He was her husband; he had bought her from her father at the auction when she was born, and she would be sent to live with him and work for him in another year or so. But now he stank of death.

In the group of men behind, Gbodi's father, his face painted yellow, held the babies. He was the village blacksmith, itself a magical employment. One baby was crying; that was the human one, which would be sacrificed to placate the other, the god child, which lay silent. Behind them the village headman, the babies' father, importantly gripped the iron fetish knife, long and heavy and black with old blood.

The juju man cast spells for their safety on all the villagers. Then, at his nod, Fola's mother-in-law and another woman went into the young woman's hut. Fola was dragged out to collapse sobbing in the centre of a circle of scared, angry faces.

The big carved message drum stood at the edge of the dancing ground, a hollowed tree-trunk with its ends covered with black goatskin. The babies were laid on it so that their blood would feed and refresh the spirit of the drum—it was hungry, for it had not had a human sacrifice for some years, only goats. More blood would paint holy patterns on the hut walls and be drunk by the women and children, while the men would eat part of the babies, to take the strength of the god into themselves. What was left would be used for strong magic later.

As the doctor began to chant again, excitement and terror filled Gbodi. She liked Fola. She felt sorry for the human baby. But they had to keep the village safe.

With a cry of triumph, the medicine man pointed towards the south-west. Already, above the furthest tree-tops, a heavy cloud was gathering. As they watched, lightning flickered across the grey. The rains were coming at last. They were doing the right thing; the gods were pleased.

Dand: Easter Mirren, near Aberdeen, Scotland. The cottage of Peter Gordon, farmer.

'It's no' the first time we've been over this; nor the twentieth. It's Dand an' Maggie for the mart this year. Now for dod's sake, Peem, give us peace!' Bessie Gordon ignored her husband's snarl, shouting him down with practised ease.

'He's but fourteen an' Maggie's no' sixteen yet. Can ye no' manage yoursel'?'

'Wi' nine bairns in the house, an' another on the drop?' Five of her own, four of her dead sister's, and never forget the smallpox babies in the churchyard . . . Bessie took a deep breath. 'Ye're no' sensible, Peem. See, Dand's done a man's work this four year. He'll get yer price for yer beasts, an' ye can warn him about cutpurses an' the like. Now save yer breath to cool yer broth!' She lumbered out, leaving her husband cursing.

Six days before, Dand and a neighbour had carried Peter in, one leg and several ribs broken by the bull and lucky to escape with his life. Bessie had grimly strapped the ribs, hauled the leg as straight as she could and splinted it. Ever since, she had known that Dand would have to drive their two fat bullocks and the fine young heifer to the Martinmas market in Aberdeen. And that her husband would resist it, with all his power.

The young ones were already standing round the table

supping their broth and barley bread. She took a small bowlful of soup, sank onto her stool by the fire, puffed with relief and lifted the sickly fourteen-month-old onto her lap to feed him. Pray God she was right, that Dand would do well for them over the three day market, and not run off to join the army like their eldest son, even the sergeant's lash less fearsome than his father's belt and the drudgery of the farm. Two years, and not a word of news, he might be dead . . . Ach, well. God guard him wherever he was.

The eldest daughter Maggie trudged in from the evening milking, wringing out her hair and shawl. 'Man, it's wild cold out! Near five gallon, ma. Thon wee red cow, dod, what a brute!'

'Kicked ye again, eh?' Bessie asked. Maggie twitched up her skirt to show the bruise under the muck on her shin. 'Tie her back leg up. Ah've told ye. Did ye wipe their udders first?'

'What harm does a bit dung in the milk do, ma? It's healthy, keeps away the smallpox.' Maggie hung up her shawl and took a bowl of broth. 'Ye have tae eat a peck o' dirt afore ye die.'

'You do what Ah tell ye, quine, an' nae argy-bargy!' her mother snapped.

'Aye, aye.' Maggie sighed. Never mind, next Hiring Fair she'd stand with the other lasses to find an employer, and be off to another farm, look for a husband, and leave young Elsie to follow her mother's daft notions . . . 'Dand's late in.'

'He's finishin' the Long Dub. A long day even for a full-grown man.' Bessie looked round the clan of children wiping their bowls with the crusts. 'Iain, you an' Jeemsie the night, eh?'

'Aye, ma!' Washing the plough ponies, feeding and watering them, cleaning their leather and chain harness, took hours of labour, but the boys all looked forward to their turn. When they finished they would sleep in the warm hayloft above, to have the team ready for Dand again before first light.

'Is it Dand for the market wi' Maggie?' Iain asked.

'Who else?' His mother snorted. 'Anybody but yer da would have seen it last week, but ye ken him . . . An' no, ye canna go wi' them! Wipe wee Rab's face for him, Morag.'

'Hooves, mam!' Jeemsie called. He and Iain headed for the door.

After a moment, it creaked open again on its leather hinges. 'Hey, Dand!' the children shouted, diving on their big brother. Small and sturdy, he staggered under the happy onslaught, grey-faced with tiredness under the mud, and tussled with them for a minute or two, trying to be as cheery as usual, before holding up his hands in surrender. 'Enough, bairns! No more games the night, Ah'm fairly beat.'

Elsie hurried to tug off Dand's soaking plaid and drape the long blanket of homespun cloth over two hooks to dry before he collapsed on a stool—not in his father's high-backed chair, never that!

'Aye, off to yer bed, the whole boilin' o' ye, an' give us some peace!' their mother ordered them. 'God guard ye while ye sleep!'

The children were ready to argue, but at Bessie's lifted hand they piled into the big box filled with heather in one corner, peering over the edge and giggling. Maggie glared. 'Get to sleep, there!' Giggling still, they drew back to settle down slowly, wriggling together like puppies under their blanket. Dand had a straw mattress in the corner opposite; Maggie and Elsie, of course, shared their parents' room.

Dand slumped against the stone wall, rubbing his swollen toes, fingers, and jug-handle ears as his chilblains burned, scrubbing a weary hand through his sweaty, carroty red hair, almost too tired to sup the broth Maggie served him.

'Dand!' A bellow from the other room. 'Did ye get that field done?'

'Aye, da!' Dand's voice was hoarse with calling to the ponies all day. 'We hit a rock, blunted the plough iron, I had to stop to sharpen it. I'll take the bairns out the morn, to lift stones—'

17

'Leave the loon take his broth!' Bessie called. She waved her son back to the stool, handed the toddler over to Elsie to put to bed and picked up the baby from its basket by the fire to feed it in its turn. She smiled at her son. Aye, Dand was a good loon. And Maggie was a sensible quine, too. They'd come to no harm in Aberdeen, whatever her man feared.

LINK TWO
Dand:
November, Aberdeen

═══════════

Broken leg or not, his father would belt the skin off his backside if he let the heifer go for less than four pounds. 'Ten pun', da says,' Dand declared. 'Fine an' healthy—never a cough nor scour.'

The farmer was screwing up his face in disgust and horror. 'Ten?' he repeated as he prodded at the heifer. 'Never! Twa pun' an' ten shillin', loon, an' a luck-penny for yersel'. There's a fair price for ye!'

Scratching his matted ginger head, Dand puffed. 'Weel— nine pun' ten, then, sir, but my da'll kill me! Her dam's the best milker in the parish—three gallon a day, regular!'

'Come awa', loon—three pun', an' that's ma best offer!'

Naturally, Dand hid his satisfaction. Not that he'd get any praise for making the price, of course. Praise to the face, certain disgrace. But if the heifer made more than expected Dand could skin a shilling or two for himself. It was a grand day!

His tattered old plaid and darned shirt and breeches did little to keep out the driving sleet of the early winter. He had carried his church-going boots to town tied to his belt, to look more respect-worthy, and his hacks and chilblains were crippling him, but it was beneath a man's dignity to pay heed to such common things as cold or sore feet; as well complain of lice, or beatings, or labour, or his gnawing hunger at the scent of hot pies wafting from an old man's basket.

The smell made Dand agree a bargain quicker than he might have done. In under an hour he and the farmer spat on their hands and shook to seal the deal; five pounds nine shillings! Delighted, Dand handed over the rope and slapped the heifer's rump in farewell, tucked two shillings carefully away into his pouch, and bought two penny pies before skipping off to where Maggie squatted among the neighbours' wives.

Though she scolded him for extravagance, she wasn't really angry; she couldn't be, not with her mouth full of hot greasy mutton. He grinned, friendly-like; she wasn't a bad wee quine, even if her eyes met each other coming and going. 'Three pound sixteen shillin' more than da said, on the three beasts. Ah'm the wee loon for the markets, eh? Have ye selled ma's cheeses?'

'Four o' them, just. An' Ah got the most o' what ma wants, an' the new seed for da.'

'Turnips, eh? Here's the siller, it'll be safer wi' ye.' As he handed over the money, Dand grinned. 'More cutpurses nor honest men in a town, da said, an' no' far wrong, Ah've seen three already! Mind my boots fur me, Ah'm aff tae see the fair.'

Hoisting her skirt to stow the coins safely in the pouch slung among her petticoats, Maggie called after him as he sidled away. 'Ye daft-like fool, Dand Gordon! Wastin' yer siller! A bearded wife, ye've seen Mistress Barr, what more d'ye want? Come back here, ye great gowk! Da'll belt ye if he finds out!'

'Weel, never tell him, then! Ah'll be back in time to mind yer cheeses so ye can slip off to the dancin'!' Chuckling, Dand trotted off among the crowd.

Some of the shows were a disappointment. A neighbour had sold a two-headed calf to gypsies the year before, the 'Smallest Woman in the World' was only an inch shorter than his own grandmother had been, and he booed the 'Strongest Man' for making more fuss about bending iron bars than Dod Murphy the smith. But the pony races along the shore were exciting, and there were jugglers and tightrope walkers, and a fire eater, and a man that ate live rats whole and then vomited them back up again, still alive and wriggling. A wife fainted, and even Dand felt queasy.

A team of Galloway wrestlers fighting all comers for a

penny tossed the country loons with ease. Two recruiting teams from rival regiments met and started fighting; one piper had his bag slit and went berserk. Three men were selling their wives, halters round their necks, all legal, the women dressed in their finest with bundles of their pots and kitchen tools, and their bedding set out at their feet to display their good workmanship. And there was a cock-fight and a badger-baiting, and a tug-o'-war, and an archery competition, and old wives selling spicy ginger and cinnamon boilings.

Near dark, Dand joined the chase yelling after a ten-year-old cutpurse till she was caught and handed over to the bailie's men, who promised, 'She'll hang the morn, ye'll see it afore ye leave!' He headed panting happily to an ale tent and found it sold not just ale, but Geneva spirit. Dand had never tasted gin before, but one man bought a round; it fairly made his ears buzz, far more than his usual quart of ale. Dod, what a day! In the happy glow he started singing with the man, who bought him another glass, or maybe two . . .

Dand rubbed at his gummy eyes. Dod, he felt . . . he wished he didn't know how he felt. He was lying on straw, thick and dry enough, in a small windowless stone room. A crack under the door let in morning grey. Like home. But not home. No place he knew. For a moment he wished for his mother. Or even for his father's belt . . . No! Shameful!

His mouth was dry and sour, and he felt sick. He tried to shout, and winced as the rasping croak hurt both his throat and his head.

Beside him the straw stirred. A head emerged. A red yawn changed to a wide grin. 'Aye, aye, loon? Ye'll be better in a wee while.' A boy, bigger than Dand, maybe sixteen, sat up, scratching absently. 'Dod, Ah'm starvin' wi' this cold! The sooner we're off to Jamaica the happier Ah'll be!'

Blearily, Dand blinked. 'Ja-Jamaica?'

'Aye, fine that.' The boy stretched, pulling straws from his matted dark hair and ragged shirt. 'We're for the Indies or Louisiana. Haste the day! How did they get ye? Pate just dropped ye inbye, an' never a word.' He caught a louse in his hair and clicked it between his thumbnails, rising to dip a horn cup in a bucket by the door. 'Are ye for a drink, loon?' he asked Dand, more kindly. 'Whit's yer name?'

'Dand—Dand Gordon.' Dand took the cup with a grunt of thirsty thanks.

'Ah'm Iain.' He refilled the cup for Dand. 'Drink up. Pate'll soon bring us our porridge, an' water to wash wi'. There's a captain comin' the day, he said.'

'A captain? What for?'

'To buy us. That's what we're here fur—to sell.'

'Sell?' He couldn't believe it.

'As indentured servants.' Iain's voice was sarcastic. 'That's what they call it. Some captain headin' for the New World, he'll buy us an' sell us off for to labour on the plantations. Five year it'll say on the ticket. Aye, that'll be right.'

'Ticket? What's that?' Dand blinked.

Iain sighed at his ignorance. 'Ye put yer mark on it—or somebody does it for ye. It says ye've agreed for to work five or six year for to pay yer passage. But they'll aye change an' change the date, to show ye're no' due freed for a year yet. Ye'll serve maybe ten year afore ye're free. An' ye canna run. Where would ye go? To live wi' the savages? An' who asked us will we or nil we, eh? Na, we're slaves.' He grinned cheerfully. 'But wi' a bit luck an' a good master, we could end up ownin' a plantation oursel's! An' at the least it'll be warm. Nae mair bliddy chilblains!'

Dand still couldn't believe it. 'Da said they done this years back. His da, my granda, his big brother an' sister was enticed away an' he never seen them again. Twenty, thirty a time they selled off. But no' now. The bailies—can they no' stop it?'

'It's the bailies as does it!' Iain jeered. 'Ah've seen them mysel', takin' the siller an' a loon or a quine bein' led awa'. Never thought about it. But when ma master died, his wife hates me, so she fetched Pate in, an' here's me.' He grinned again. 'Ach, worse happens in war. Ah dinnae have to work for my meat. An' Pate'll no' beat ye just for pleasure, like Annie done. How did he get ye?'

'Ah drove beasts in for the mart. An' there was the fair.' Iain nodded. Nobody would leave without seeing the sights. 'An' a man buyed me a drink or two an' Ah waked up here.'

'A big red-faced brute, great fat han's thick wi' black hair?' Dand nodded. 'Pate. That'll learn ye, eh? An have ye yer siller yet?'

'Aye, he didnae get that.' Dand almost grinned. 'Ah'd spent what pence Ah had, an' ma sister Maggie has the main part safe—Dod, she'll be fair demented missin' me!' The thought gave him a faint hope. 'Ah'll have the law on them!'

Outside, there were sounds of movement, of a key in the lock. With a screech the door slammed open. The boys blinked, wincing at the light. A tall, heavy-set man came in, a whip in his hand; the man who had bought the drink. 'Aye, Pate!' Iain chirped.

Unspeaking, Pate jerked his head. Iain skipped out readily, but Dand hesitated till Pate whipped him out into a narrow yard surrounded by high walls. Even if he had felt well enough to struggle, Dand could never have escaped.

Outside, two other men, well dressed and clean, studied the boys with exactly the same expression the farmer had used when examining the heifer. Before that indifferent stare Dand lost all his little defiance and stood dumb while he was poked, his muscles felt, his mouth forced open by a rough thumb for his teeth to be examined.

'Aye, the big loon's no' bad. What's your name, son? Have ye a trade?'

'Iain Boag, sir. Four year workin' tae a cooper, sir,' Iain answered smartly.

The man nodded. 'Good, good. But the other—well . . . '

The fat one eased a silver snuff-box from a tight pocket. 'A fine sturdy farm loon, Captain Maxwell, sir. Fit for years o' work on a plantation, years.' He took a pinch of snuff, sneezing mightily.

'Aye, maybe that, sir. Small, though.'

'Ach, he's young yet. About twelve or so.'

'Ah'm near fifteen!' Dand protested, and yelped as Pate's whip cut his bare calves.

'No, let him be!' Maxwell looked pleased. The other man didn't. 'Fourteen, eh? He'll no' grow much more.' He made them trot up and down the yard like ponies. 'Can ye read an' write?' Iain shook his head, but Maxwell looked disgusted as Dand nodded. 'Aye, well, that's bad. Few will buy a lawyer, aye arguin' an' makin' trouble. Ye've nae others, sir?'

'No' the now, captain!' The fat man shrugged regretfully. 'It's no' like the old days. But this pair's fine loons, an' profitable, eh? Mind, ye're before yer time, sir. They're no' lookin' their best.'

The captain grinned. 'That's why I came early. Aye. Uhuh. How much, sir?'

'To you, Captain Maxwell, a regular—ten pun' the wee loon, fifteen the big.'

The captain snorted with contempt. 'I'd no' get that for them in Jamaica. Two an' three.'

The fat man winced theatrically. 'Ye'll bankrupt me, sir!'

'Bankrupt a bailie? It's no' possible!' Maxwell laughed heartily.

Dand's heart sank. Iain was right enough. It was the magistrates who were running the kidnapping trade.

Iain was grinning perkily. The fat man smiled fondly. 'See him, sir, fair itchin'—' He broke off.

From a distance a hoarse voice floated over the wall. 'Dand! Are ye there, Dandy! Has anybody seen a lost loon? Dand Gordon! Where are ye? Dand!'

Maggie! Dand took a breath—but before he could yell, Pate's huge hand was clamped across his mouth, smothering him back against the man's greasy waistcoat, helpless to shout or even to breathe, his bare feet kicking vainly against Pate's leather-gaitered shins.

'Aye, good man!' They all stood silent as Maggie's frantic crying passed along the street outside and faded.

Smiling gently, the fat man nodded to Pate. Dand was dropped, gasping and sobbing, while the bailie raised a reassuring hand. 'Never fear, Captain Maxwell, there's nothin' the quine could do, even if she found the loon. I'd say he'd been arrested for drunken assault, or whatever. There's naebody can argue wi' a bailie. But less bother if we keep it to oursel's, eh? She'll likely think he's gone for a soldier. Now—what was it we said?'

Dand shuddered in terror and despair. Would he ever see Maggie again?

They finally settled on five pounds for Dand, and seven for Iain. 'Ach, ye're a hard man, sir!' But as they shook hands on the deal, the fat man didn't seem too upset.

Dand felt empty. He was worth less than his heifer.

The waistband of Dand's breeches was cut, so that his hands were kept busy holding them up. 'Ye'll no' try runnin', will ye?' Pate warned the boys, hefting his whip. 'Ah'm right behind ye!'

'Nae fear, sir! No' me!' Grinning, Iain led the way to the gate and marched gaily down the street behind the captain.

Desperately Dand looked for Maggie or any of his friends; but among all the crowds, there was no one he knew. If he ducked under that wagon horse's nose he'd be away . . . Before he could twitch, a loop of the whip noosed his neck. 'Forget it,' Pate growled. 'Get on!'

At the quayside Pate hustled the boys up a gangplank, among jostling sailors, down a ladder and into a black cupboard half full of ropes. The door slammed.

Distant shouting. Feet stamping above them. Creaking. The ship began to rock gently.

'We're off!' Iain exulted. 'Cheer up, loon, at least ye'll never see Pate again!'

In the pitch dark rats began to rustle and squeak, just as in the byre at home. Dand at last began to cry.

LINK THREE
Juliet:
November—January, Liverpool

First, Juliet had to convince her horrified brother. 'You'd ruin your reputation! No respectable woman would speak to you! And who'd ever marry you?'

She sniffed. 'Who'll marry me now, with this nose, except a fortune-hunter? But I'll never marry. All a wife's property belongs to her husband. I'll never let that happen!'

'Never marry? But . . . ' He could scarcely credit it. A husband to look after her and deal with all her affairs, give her a home and children, rank and wealth, was surely the goal of every woman's life! 'That's unnatural! And improper!'

'Improper! That's what old people say to stop girls having any fun. I've worn your clothes lots of times, for the cock-fights and so on, and that wasn't proper either.'

'I should never have let you persuade me! No!'

'Nobody realized I wasn't a boy!'

'This is different—you'd be found out! On board a ship everybody lives on top of everybody else, sharing cabins—'

'The owner's son, and supercargo? Of course you'll get a cabin of your own. I'll manage.'

'It's a slaving trip, Juliet! It'll be ghastly!'

'You threw up at that prize-fight, not me.' Although her stomach squirmed at the memory of blood and teeth on the grass, this couldn't be much worse!

'No! You could be seasick, or die!'

'So could you! Dying would solve the problems of the one who dies, anyway.' Her eyes sparkled with merriment at Anthony's appalled face. 'And seasickness would cover any differences people might notice.'

'Will you listen to me? No!' her brother protested weakly. 'I'll tell papa!'

'You do and I'll slay you! And tell him about you taking me to the prize-fight!' As his resistance collapsed, she smiled at him. 'We can do it, Tony! Yes, we can! Now, think. Your fees for your tuition and keep are paid for this year, aren't they? But you'll need spending money—and so will I. Grandmama says I have to organize it all myself—she won't help, not with money. H'm. I've got an ancient, hideous ring of great-grandmama's. I'll never wear it, but it has a fine ruby. You can sell it.'

'What about Miss Lazenby? When you don't arrive she'll write to find out why.'

'Well thought of!' she encouraged him, as if he was starting to take an active part in the planning. 'Um . . . I'll write a letter on papa's notepaper saying I'm ill and won't be coming this year, but she is to retain the fees for next year. That will keep her happy.'

'How will you get away? Papa will send you in a post-chaise—maybe go with you himself—'

'He's far too busy. I'll find a way, trust me!'

'I don't!'

'You must! I need to leave just before you sail. But we can do it! You'll have to do the organizing outside, I'm not allowed out alone, girls are so tied down! But I can stay with grandmama, she'll do that much for me. Then just before you sail, you can slip away to say goodbye to her, as you might well do anyway, and I'll go back instead of you. They'll be too busy to see any difference.'

'But if papa finds out? Or if it all goes wrong?'

'Oh, Tony! Don't be such a bubble-baby! They'll know eventually, after all. If for any reason we can't change places, we're no worse off than now. And they won't disinherit us! Mama will have the vapours again, which could help us, you know how it annoys papa till he'll do the exact opposite of whatever she wants.' Anthony blinked; he had never realized that.

'Papa will rage as usual.' He shuddered. 'Oh, cheer up! It doesn't do any harm except to your ears. But they can't

28

actually disinherit us, or anything too drastic.' She hoped. Last month papa had had her held down over a table by the maids and caned for impertinence, and this would be worse. 'Can you see mama letting her catty friends know about such a scandal? Or papa, at the Corn Exchange? But we'll succeed, you'll end up a bishop, and I'll run the firm and make you a marvellous income!'

Or at the very least she would have one adventure to remember . . .

Like a good sister, she supervised the making and packing of Tony's clothes for the voyage. 'Quiet colours, that won't draw the eye. Not that emerald waistcoat with the gold— it's far too gaudy!' A dozen shirts and neckcloths. Two dozen pairs of black silk stockings. She could use them monthly, and wash them out herself; anyone who noticed a bloodstain would think it was from a burst blister. She had most of the smallclothes made in linen, not wool, in spite of her nurse's arguments that it would be unhealthy. It would all fit well enough, even the boots.

Luckily, the times fitted also. She was to begin school at the beginning of January; the *Kestrel* would be refitted and stocked, ready to sail, only a week later.

'What have you done today? Tell me all about the officers. How do you reach your cabin? How is the cargo stowed?' she questioned Anthony every night.

'You're worse than the Spanish Inquisition!' he protested.

'I need to know! So tell me!' She grinned. 'Besides, isn't papa pleased with the way you're attending to your work!'

Her greatest worry was about her escape from the journey to Bath. Mama insisted she must have a maid and a manservant as escort, as well as John Coachman. How could she evade them without papa being told instantly? Juliet racked her brains in vain; and then, at the last moment, she was lucky.

Just after the Christmas celebrations, she was curled in a big chair by the library window reading *Travels to Discover the Source of the Nile*, the only book on Africa she could find—did the blackamoors really eat raw meat?—when a little maid staggered in with a brass scuttle of coal. Not noticing Juliet, she knelt on the hearthrug to make up the fire, and to Juliet's astonishment began to cry.

'What's wrong?' Unlike her mother, Juliet noticed the maids. 'You're new, aren't you?'

At the first word the girl started up in alarm, sniffling and rubbing at her raw nose with a red-knuckled hand. 'Polly, missus, that's us, just come last month. Fourth under-'ouse-maid. It's us back, see, thon wicked coal-scuttles, an' no rest, not if ever so, an' there's cans o' water for baths, up three floors, an' hurry, hurry to keep 'em hot, not if ever so, an' the steps to scrub, an' the pots till after midnight an' then up at four for to make below-stairs breakfast at half five.' Juliet blinked. She had not realized how hard a skivvy worked for her two shillings a week. And her keep, of course. 'Missus Goldsmiff she says no rest for the wicked, she says, but us ain't not wicked, not if ever so, an' thon other maids, puts on us they does, an' the black men, an'—'

'Stop snivelling, Polly! How old are you? Nine? Well, you're old enough to know you've been engaged for a year. I promise you, by that time you'll feel much happier.' As the little girl whimpered, Juliet frowned. 'Do you want to go home to your mother till your back is better?'

'Neh!' The girl cast her a look of pure scorn. 'No room, see, missus. Twenty-two on us in the cellar, see, wi' the littl'uns an' me dad—lost both 'ands in the army, 'e's got 'ooks but it ain't the same—an' Auntie Gussie an' 'er lads an' Uncle Jimmy an' 'is woman an' 'er bairns, see, an' the lodger an' 'is, but one's nobbut a babe—' Struggling to follow the thick accent Juliet thought, Hooks for hands? A lodger in a cellar? Lud! 'An' the gutter runnin' horseshit down the steps when it rains, never dry nor clean, not if ever so, an' the rats eatin' the bairns, see?' Juliet shuddered as the girl pushed back her cap to show half an ear. 'Mam told us to get out.' She sniffed and swiped her nose again, gathering her courage. 'Us'll get on, see. Work us way up.'

'You want to be a cook? Or a lady's maid? Or marry?' Mama always complained that no sooner had she trained a maid than the dratted girl went off and wed some handsome young footman or visiting tradesman.

'Neh! 'Ousekeeper like Missus Goldsmiff, that's us, an' everybody scared on us, like 'er!'

Juliet smiled at the fierce ambition in the infant's eye. 'I'm sure you'll make it! But the fires are the footmen's work. Did they tell you to do it? Idle dollops! Mrs Goldsmith would be angry, did you tell her?' Polly gaped; speak to the awesome housekeeper? She'd not dare! Juliet tutted. 'How can she help if she doesn't know? You—no, I'll tell her, and she'll tell the steward, and he'll warm their lazy black hides for them.'

The girl's face showed both gratitude and doubt as Juliet jumped up. She ignored the look; yes, the housekeeper's attitudes to a grubby little skivvy and to one of the young ladies would be very different, and quite right too. 'Come along! Don't worry, I'll tell her not to scold you for letting yourself be seen by the Family.' Nine years old! Scarcely out of the cradle! But the girl just had to learn to cope.

The footmen, Pompey and Samson, were her mother's slaves, a wedding gift from papa as little black pageboys. When they grew up mama had kept them on instead of sending them off to be sold in Jamaica to a plantation, as happened to many young blacks before they could realize they were officially free in Britain and start getting uppity. They sneered arrogantly at everyone in all their glory of gold-braided maroon livery and powdered wigs. A beating would do them good.

However, to everyone's annoyance they sulked after it, looming about the house like sullen brown thunderclouds, glowering stiff-faced, awesomely correct. Drat them, Juliet thought! She had a good mind to order it repeated, for sheer insolence!

Six days before her departure Juliet had almost given up hope of escape and was resignedly finishing packing her school trunk. Then the usual milkman, who brought them a safe supply straight from his own cows, didn't turn up. The cook sent a maid out to buy from a street milkmaid carrying a couple of open buckets on a yoke. Her milk was old and stale, dusty with dry dung from the streets and gritty with muck, watered down from a dirty well, with crushed snails in it to make it look frothy and fresh.

Half the household fell ill of typhoid, including Juliet's younger sisters and John Coachman.

Mama fluttered round, sprinkling the sickroom with lavender water, disturbing the children, getting in Nurse's way, demanding that Juliet stay to help, then ordering her to leave at once before she too fell ill. In the end Mister Smethwick, infuriated by the turmoil, hired a post-chaise and pair. 'Dear God, your mother would drive a saint to drink! I have three ships in to attend to, and no time for this nonsense. You'll take one of the maids and the blacks and leave tomorrow, Juliet.'

Juliet's heart hurt with a sudden leap of joy. Mama was too distraught to pay attention. Papa didn't know the maids. She knew just which one she wanted!

By six o'clock next morning she was bowling out of Liverpool on the London Road, wrapped in a hooded thick-furred cape, her feet on oven-heated bricks in the straw on the carriage floor, a hot stone in her muff. On the seat in front of her sat Polly, hands tight clasped on her lap, well warned how to behave, and alternately giggling in sheer rapture and overawed by the responsibility. Pompey and Samson clung behind on the box, shivered and froze in the biting wind despite heavy overcoats and mufflers, and cursed her. Ahead, the postilion riding the left-hand horse urged his mount and its partner into a canter down the rough, muddy road.

At the very first stop to change horses, Juliet knocked on the roof for the footmen to let down the steps. 'I need a hot cup of chocolate, and the bricks re-heated. Here's a shilling—you may take a drink too. I shall be half an hour.'

Considering how the blacks were feeling, they'd make the most of her silly, apparently ignorant permission.

Polly protested nervously. 'Miss, they'll be fuddled as fiddlers! "Drunk for a penny, dead drunk for twopence," gin-houses says.'

'Sh! Yes, I know!' This was where it might still go all wrong . . . 'Polly, can I trust you? In something very, very important?'

'Ooh, aye, miss!' The little girl was puzzled but emphatic. 'Anythin', miss!'

'Thank you.' Touched by the unexpected loyalty, Juliet almost hugged the child. 'In a while I'll call them, scold them for being drunk, and say I've met a friend and we'll go on with her. I'll tell them to go back and repay papa the rest of the hire fee. Will they do that, do you think?'

Polly shook her head knowingly. 'Neh, they'll skive off for the three days, miss, an' keep the brass. Might not never go back, them blacks. Talkin' big about runnin' off to Lunnon—says they's blackamoors there'll take 'em in, find 'em work.'

Juliet hesitated. She hadn't meant her father to lose two valuable servants . . . but they would probably stay where they were well off. 'Anyway, papa won't hear about it, not for days.'

Polly guffawed. 'An' whatever happens to 'em when 'e do find out, serve 'em right, sozzlin' sots! What's us gonner do, then, missus? Er—miss?'

'We'll go back to Liverpool. There's a coach goes by in about an hour. But to my grandmother, not home again. I'm going away, but you can stay there. Don't go back to Bold Street! If papa finds you—'

'Find us? Never, miss!'

'Good. But just in case—' In case grandmama died, though she couldn't say so. 'I'll write you a letter explaining that you've acted under my orders, and a letter of recommendation if you want to seek a new position.'

Polly's expression was a ridiculous mixture of horror and glee. 'Eh, miss—you elopin'?'

'What? Oh. I can't say.' This would make Polly feel helpful.

'Can't us come too, miss? Ye'll need a maid!'

'No, I'm afraid not. But when I have a house of my own, I'll take you on again, I promise, and you'll end up as my housekeeper.' As Polly opened her mouth to argue, Juliet played the clincher. 'I'll give you three pounds, Polly, and you can have my trunk and keep the clothes or sell them.' They were far too big for the child, of course, but they could be cut down, or in the flea market the new, quality clothes would fetch a small fortune.

'All the lace an' all? Ooh!' Overwhelmed by this amazing generosity, Polly declared fervently, 'Yer can trust us, missus! Us'll none say nowt t'yer da—er—I'll keep it quiet, miss! An' us—er—I wishes yer every 'appiness an' success, miss!'

Happiness and success—she certainly hoped so!

LINK FOUR
Hassan:
December

―――――

'The Hadith beginning, "If you see a wrong."' The rows of boys cross-legged on rugs on the sandy yard of the old madrassah all looked eager—this was one of the teacher's favourite sayings of the Prophet. 'Hassan?'

Hassan rose confidently. ' "If you see a wrong being done you should stop it with your hand. If you cannot use your hand, then stop it with your tongue. If you cannot speak out against it, then at least you should hate it in your heart. And that is the weakest of faith." '

'Good. Remember it always on your journey.'

'I will, sir, I will!' Sitting again in the front row, Hassan sighed in sheer joy as he felt his friends' envious stares on his back. What luck he had, to be leaving the next day on such a wonderful adventure, his future bright when he returned and studied to become a respected teacher himself—ah, Allah and Muhammad, blessings and peace be on His name, were smiling on him!

When lessons ended at noon, Hassan stalked proudly out to meet his father, short and dignified in his white djellaba and embroidered red hat. Sedately he followed him for the midday prayer into the vast, shadowy mosque with its multitude of small spires, and then, with a sweeping, breathless delight, on to a world of new experiences.

Every afternoon, Uzum had been taking his son with him to the hundreds of meetings and discussions needed to arrange the journey east. Hassan had been introduced to the homes of merchants and scribes, soldiers, craftsmen and boatmen, True Believers and pagans, freemen and slaves; to tiled mosques, thatched huts, cool, arcaded halls and dim, spicy warehouses, all much patched, for every year their mud-brick walls were damaged by the winter rains. Djenne was not the city it had been in its glorious past, when it had rivalled the great Timbuktu as a trading and university centre for the vast Songhai kingdom, but it was still large, and every need could be filled here.

Uzum was an experienced and respected trader, who easily found four partners. Among them they employed several guards, many with useful languages of the tribes they would be passing through. Desert Tuaregs, tall and blue-veiled, their sword-hilts sticking high above their shoulders, would be useless on the river. Most of the guards were Hausa, like Hassan and his family, or Bambara; two were tall, elegant southern Fantis and two Yoruba from the east. They had a few slaves as cooks and servants, including Hassan's best friend, his father's lad Dawud, and an Ibo from far to the east where the Great River was said to meet the sea. The whole party was almost forty people.

The guards had their own weapons. Uzum bought plenty of powder and shot, and for Hassan, to his ecstatic joy, a long, slim musket, engraved and inlaid with mother-of-pearl.

To buy slaves and ivory and hire guides and interpreters, and as presents for the kings and chiefs, Uzum would carry sacks of cowries, the usual river coinage; amber, brass, and glass jewellery; cotton and silk cloths; brass cups and pots; embroidered and tasselled leather bags and saddles and scented cushions; slabs of salt, precious as gold, brought on camel-back from the desert salt mines; inlaid swords and daggers; a small bag of gold coins and a telescope.

On the day of departure the imam came to Farouk's house to lead special prayers for their success and safety. They began, as always at the start of a journey, with the Opening, the first chapter of the Koran. 'In the Name of God, the Merciful, the Compassionate . . . Thee only we serve; to Thee alone we pray for succour. Guide us in the straight path . . . ' The whole Koran would have been repeated many times over by the time they returned.

At length the straggling, noisy procession of men, horses, camels, mules, and flea-bitten donkeys set off past the Great Mosque towards the river. Uzum smiled as he eyed the dancing, cheering mob shouting, blowing trumpets, beating drums, clashing bells and cymbals. 'If they paddle with this much energy, we'll be back in a month!'

More or less veiled, all the women clustered to see them off on Farouk's flat roof, leaning out between the yellow buttresses like cows' horns along the front, shrilling long, wailing trills of grief and glory. Hassan waved back. His grandmother was waving at the front. 'Bridie Treworthy!' he yelled to her, forgetting his dignity. She had been dinning it into him every night, with her few remembered words of English. He scarcely believed that they would find any white men, though his father was confident. 'Turo, Cornal!'

They turned a corner round a high wall, and his home was hidden.

No more school, no more Taranah, not for months. He was free!

By the crowded wharves the boats bought for the voyage were waiting, already loaded; four dugout canoes, the smallest forty feet long, each of two large treetrunks hollowed out and fastened end to end. Each held a ton or so of goods, with about ten professional paddlers of the Bozo tribe and a dozen traders and guards. Over the centre of each boat a canvas awning was raised on hoops. Hassan was far too excited to go into the shelter; he settled in the high-jutting bows of the lead boat, beside the lookout. Beside him Dawud cheerfully squeezed in as well.

'Sit still, and don't fall in or the crocodiles will eat you for breakfast!' the lookout growled at them, but he was only pretending gruffness. The two youngsters exchanged a grin.

At last, after more prayers, after the last message had been shouted, after the final extra parcel had been tossed aboard, in a din of drums and cheers, bells and trumpets and musket shots, the canoes pushed away from the wharf. Hassan and Dawud's friends shrilled farewell. The master boatman started a steady drum-beat, the paddlers picked up the rhythm with a grunt and deep-throated chant, and the long boats shot out into the current.

This first part of the journey was familiar. Hassan had been out before with his father or his uncle's men, carrying grain and fruit to and from outlying farms along the river. The brown water curling and swirling along the canoe's painted sides and the slight breeze of their passage made boating almost a cool way to travel on even the hottest of days. Now, in the cold mist of Sahara dust with which the harmattan wind filled the air, it was warming.

For many kilometres irrigated fields stretched back from the river, green from the rains, with shadoofs dip-dipping their leather sacks of water into the ditches, the black skins of their workers shining in the sunshine as they paused to watch the flotilla of long boats drive past. Camels swayed and donkeys trudged solemnly along under immense loads, or rested with their owners in the shade of thorn trees and palms. An occasional horseman cantered along, waving cheerfully.

Gradually, though, the banks changed as they moved away from the safety of the city, into the less-travelled part of the river. Sand swallowed the fields and huts; the thorn bushes crept closer to the water; finally all sign of people vanished into a general open, sparse landscape of bushes and sand, with crocodiles basking on the sandbanks along the shore. Here, men built their huts back from the river, away from flooding, hidden from attack.

The elderly lookout gave Hassan and Dawud poles to help shove the canoe aside from sandbars or snags. 'You youngsters have sharp eyes. That swirl and ripple is a sunken tree. It could hole a canoe. That change in the colour of the water, and the curl in the current, is a sandbank. It has been there for six years, but it could be swept away during the rains, and a new one built anywhere.' True; only an hour later, the canoes met an unexpected sandbar, and it took three hours and a lot of sweating, grunting labour to lighten them, shove them over the shallow to deeper water, reload and continue.

After six days without any worse accident, just before the sudden dark they grounded the canoes at a well-known camp-site on a small island, safe from attack in the middle of a wide lake. 'How far have we gone, father?'

'The day after tomorrow we'll reach Kambara, the port for Timbuktu,' Uzum said. 'But then it may be five or ten times as far again to the ocean.' Hassan puffed in awe as his father laughed. 'Allowing for grounding and accidents, illness, stops for rest and haggling, it could be three months before you taste salt in the water! But what is written is written.'

The routine of setting up camp was fairly smooth by now. After five hours crouched in the canoe since the noon stop, Hassan's legs were cramped rigid, but Dawud rubbed them easy. With their poles the two boys beat the bushes all round to drive away any snakes, and checked for crocodile nests near the camp. 'Remember,' Uzum called, 'if you see hippos, leave them alone! Come and tell us and we'll bring torches to drive them back into the water.'

Several fires were quickly started and mealies and goat stew set to cook, even before the tents were set up. Dawud grinned at Hassan. 'What a din! No hippo will come near us!'

Hassan smiled back. '*Inshallah.*'

'God is most Great! God is most Great!' While they were travelling, the five daily prayers were combined into two sessions, one before they set out and one in the evening. Now the man chosen to lead the prayers for the journey was calling them to prayer.

Dawud looked round. 'Are the prayer mats still in the boats?'

'I'll give you a hand,' Hassan offered. The boys spread the mats out on the bank before hurrying down to the river to wash among the rest, to purify themselves for the prayer.

The boatmen, who were mostly pagans, stayed beside their own fires.

'There is no god but God!' the muezzin called. Shaking water from his hands, Hassan stepped on to his mat between his father and Dawud, and turned to the north-east, towards Mecca. Together they made the prescribed movements of prayer, sank to their knees to touch their foreheads to the ground—and suddenly Dawud screamed, holding his calf. 'Scorpion!' In the red sunset light his black face was grey with shock and fear.

Hassan gasped, 'Father! Dawud—'

His father was already shoving him aside, lifting the boy bodily and running with him towards the nearest fire. 'A brand—quickly!' he snapped to the cook. With his knife Uzum slashed across Dawud's leg, three gashes so deep that the bone showed through, stabbed his knife into the sand, with one hand grabbed Dawud's foot and with the other the burning stick the cook offered him, and thrust the flaming end down into the cuts he had made. 'Another brand! And another!' Though Dawud screamed and writhed, some men hurrying to help held him still while Uzum thoroughly cauterized the wounds.

Hassan smashed the scorpion into the ground. It must have been trapped under the mat, and struck as it wriggled free. Why couldn't it have respected their prayers and just scuttled away?

At last Uzum relaxed slightly. 'We'll put on a poultice of water-weeds, and bandage it up now. Thank you, Mohammed, Ali. That is all we can do. All things are in the hands of God.'

Hassan had already found the strips of cotton that his father had brought for bandages. Some of the merchants were finishing their prayers, paying no attention. How could they? Angry, he splashed into the water, careless of possible snakes or crocodiles, to grope for a bundle of water-weeds. Uzum nodded to him. 'Well done, son! A good pad on the cuts—that's right.'

'Will I die, sir?' Dawud sobbed.

'Die? Allah is All-Merciful and Compassionate. A fever, a sore leg for a few days, yes. But die? Rubbish!' Uzum patted the boy's shoulder gently. 'Lie still now, and my son will soon nurse you well, eh?' However, though his voice was comforting, the glance he gave Hassan held little hope. 'Come, my son. Let us finish our prayers, and make an extra prayer for Dawud.'

Hassan prayed very hard, but Dawud died before noon the next day, whispering, 'There is no god but God.'

As Dawud's friend, Hassan led the prayers at the burial. 'O Allah, give him an abode more excellent than his abode was here, with a family better than his family, and a companion better than his companion . . . ' He had known Dawud all his life, had been brought up with him, fought and played with him, been closer to him than to his best friends at school. Dawud had not asked to come on this voyage. Hassan wept for him. So did his father.

It wasn't a good start to the journey.

Dand:
December, Scotland

After hours of damp black cold, Dand and Iain were led up swaying ladders to blink on the deck. Above them dirty brownish sails spread squares and triangles in the afternoon grey, and sailors were being driven by shouting to heave barrels and ropes around.

From the raised poop deck, three steps high, Captain Maxwell eyed them without favour. 'Aye, well. You—' to Iain '—ye'll work with the carpenter. Now you. Dand, is it? Aye. Ever been on a ship afore?'

'No, sir.' Dand shook his head. It was the final straw for his queasy stomach. He dashed for the side of the ship; unfortunately, upwind. The deck was well splattered.

'Ye'll kiss the gunner's daughter for that, ye villain!' A dozen blows with a knotted rope's end made sure the boy remembered to puke downwind in future.

Dand was small, and totally ignorant of the multitude of skills a sailor needed. 'Waste o' time teachin' ye the ropes,' Maxwell declared. 'I'll be selling ye in three months. Ye'll be cabin boy.'

Easing his breeches off the welts on his backside, Dand perked up. An easy job that, eh?

In some ways, he was right. He had to clean the captain's big cabin, all of four metres long and three wide, fetch Maxwell's food, have dry clothing and hot coffee always ready for when his master came off watch wet and cold. He lived fairly dry, with a hanging charcoal stove and a painted floor-cloth, instead of huddling in the dank forecastle among the rest of the crew. To add to the normal porridge or peasemeal, maggoty cheese or half-boiled gristle that went by the name of salt beef, he could steal left-over food from the captain's dishes. He worked less, and ate as well as at home.

But he kissed the gunner's daughter for any fault, any slowness, any awkwardness. Or none.

Worst were the evenings. After dinner Dand shrank into stillness in his corner while Maxwell settled down at his desk with a pot of coffee, his quill pens, and books of Greek. 'Time for my intellectual exercise, eh, lad? Ah, Homer—greatest o' them all. An' *The Odyssey*—a sailor's tale, eh?' The captain was making a new translation of the Greek epic, without using the letter 'p'; a lipogram, it was called, he told Dand proudly. But it was difficult; names often included the hated letter. Let too many p's appear, and Maxwell's face would contort in frustration. Then, if Dand caught his eye, 'I'll learn you to sit still!'—or keep the coffee hot, or not stare, or whatever—and Maxwell reached for the knotted rope on its hook by the door.

Dand clenched his teeth and bore it. Intellectual exercise? Even his father wasn't this bad. He learned that the last boy had died during three weeks of calm in the Doldrums.

He also learned not to whistle on deck, along with a hundred other superstitions. When a gale blew up, he was beaten again for calling it.

He wasn't alone, of course. All the sailors were driven to work with a rope's end or a hard fist. Moving too slowly, grumbling too loud, even looking sullen could get you a savage beating.

Iain was philosophic. 'They can aye jump ship. But they're clad an' fed, nae worries but the weather an' the captain's temper, an' there's plenty worse nor Maxwell. Aye, there's bad days, but where are there no', eh? An' there's foreign ports an' women, an' they can trade for theirsel's, make a bit siller, eh? An' dream on a lucky bit salvage or piracy to let them buy a farm or marry an innkeeper's widow an' live like a gentleman. No' a bad life, eh?'

North and then west they struggled through storm and raging waves. For a week Dand was wretchedly sick, not that it saved him any work, or beatings. But at last they dropped anchor in the Kyle of Tongue on the north coast of Scotland.

On flat ground by the shore were camped nearly two hundred thin, worn folk of all ages from babies to white-headed ancients of fifty, huddled in ramshackle huts of the local flat slate piled into crude walls and roofed with turfs or plaids on a scaffolding of driftwood.

'Broken folks. Emigrants for the Americas. The carpenter told me.' Iain gazed at the ragtag crowd, rising sluggishly from beside tiny seaweed fires to shuffle to the shore in eerie silence. Some smiled; others wept. 'Half starved. Cleared off their land, see, to let in the sheep.'

'Aye, aye.' Dand nodded. It was happening all over. To improve the land, and their rents, many lairds evicted their half-starved clansfolk, and burned their houses behind them or even over their heads. 'Sheep pay better, eh? That's how da got our farm. It kept five houses afore him. Dozy Highland scruffs couldn't even speak English.' But Dand felt a sudden, unexpected pity. What had happened to the folk his father had displaced? Da told, laughing, of how some had tried to hide, but had been hunted out with dogs and dragged aboard the ships in chains. Had some escaped to the factories in the southern towns? Or just starved to death? Had they all been lazy and ignorant?

'Captain Maxwell?' A man in a clerical gown and white neck-bands, rather better-fed than the others, was bobbing in a tiny boat by the ship's side. 'You were due here in August! The people have eaten their oatmeal that was to feed them on the voyage. What has kept you?'

'God's will, reverend!' Maxwell drew himself up impressively. 'Unless the Lord send a favourable wind, a ship cannot even leave harbour. I regret the delay, sir, but we are here now. You may come aboard at once.' He smiled like a shark. 'Anticipatin' the need, reverend sir, I aye carry oatmeal to sell to my passengers.'

Dand grimaced. He knew that meal. It was damp and mouldy, more maggots and grit than meal, more rye than oats, but Maxwell would charge high for it. Good business, for him.

The *Daisy*'s hold was under two metres high, twenty-four long, and seven wide in the centre. Light came from the hatchway above, and two small candle lanterns. Along each side were built triple tiers of wooden shelves under two metres square, each shelf split into two bunks by a narrow plank set on edge. Head-room and the spaces between the stacks were barely an arm's length. Boxes and bundles were tossed down the hatch by the sailors for the emigrants to sort out themselves, and stack in the centre of the hold as seats and extra sleeping area.

Dand was set to direct the folk as they climbed down the ladder. 'A family in each bunk.' They could take turns sleeping. The Gaelic-speaking emigrants, flustered and lost, gazed blankly. 'Dod, can ye no' understan' me, ye gowks?'

The emigrants' three cows, tugged swimming behind the ship's boat to be lifted aboard by rope slings, mooing helplessly, head and legs dangling, were penned at one end of the hold with a few armfuls of grass for fodder. They settled quicker than the folk, but there was less din than Dand had expected. The women did not squabble. They hung plaids and shawls, dresses and petticoats as bunk curtains to create a suggestion of privacy, or argued for more space, but dispiritedly. Even the children's crying was weak. Apathetic in despair, many people simply collapsed on the bare boards.

Astonishingly soon, driven on by the mate and a fair wind, the *Daisy* was away again. The emigrants clung to the rail, staring back, weeping, wailing, unheeding the minister's comforting, hopeful prayers.

Dand sneered. 'Dod, are they no' dismal, just?' he muttered to Iain. 'Aye, they're grieved to leave their homes, but at least they're goin' to be their own masters. No' like us!' Unwarily he shrugged, winced, and ran below; the captain would soon be looking for coffee.

That day was their last fair wind. Against the westerly

gales the *Daisy* tacked north and south, inching forward till a sail's worn canvas would split, a yard would crack or a fraying rope would snap, and she would be driven east again until the fault was repaired; over and over. It was too dangerous to light the galley fire, so that everything was eaten raw—oatmeal, pease, even the salt meat. Thirst tormented them all.

By the eighth day two babies and an old man had died, of cold and exhaustion.

After two weeks, during a woman's funeral, her daughter threw herself and her baby overboard, the shout and splash half lost in the howl of the wind. Unable to bear the unending din, the howl of the wind in the ropes and the creaking and crashing of the wooden ship; the never-resting rolling and pitching; the sludge of sea water, vomit, urine, filth that washed ankle-deep through the black, rat-infested hell of the hold; the hunger and wet cold, stink and weeping, seasickness and despair at the loss of all the world she knew, the young woman had lost the courage to go on.

In the tossing, five men and eleven women emigrants, five children and three sailors broke bones or dislocated joints. A sail had split into shreds in the gale, and a sailor trying to replace it, fighting the stiff canvas that flapped like demons' wings, was flung from the yardarm and vanished instantly in the surf.

The ship sprang a leak. Instead of merely an hour or two daily, the pump clanked endlessly, every man including the emigrants driven to gut-splitting labour heaving at the handles, tied to the pump against the waves that rolled green over the decks. A man was swept away, tangled in the ropes set up to stop the crew from being washed overboard, and drowned in front of their eyes.

The minister came to beg Maxwell to turn back. Furious, Maxwell snarled, 'I'm paid to carry ye to Boston, sir. Would ye have me break my given word? Get below! Mister Robb! Fasten down the hatch! It's I am master of this vessel, no' the passengers!'

The captain's temper worsened, but he had to spend so much time on deck that he was exhausted and Dand was beaten less. In disgusted pity, the boy tried to help the exiles, carrying buckets of water down to them, emptying the brimming latrine barrel, and reassuring them that yes, they would soon be in America, soon, soon.

But the marks on the chart in the cabin showed that the ship was making no progress.

Then three people died in one day. Of ship fever; typhus. The killer.

Captain Maxwell sat at his desk that evening, glowering at the chart. Behind him Dand kept tensely still. 'To hell wi' this!' Maxwell pushed himself to his feet, pausing at the door to stare threateningly at Dand. 'Ye'll no' speak to the passengers again!' He went out. 'All hands!' A stumble of weary feet, cracking thuds and yelps as ropes' ends drove the exhausted men to work, a heavy creaking as the rudder was put over and the sails reset. For a few minutes the *Daisy* rolled violently, turning across the waves, and then settled to a slower, less frenzied heave. Even Dand could feel that she was running more easily.

But he looked at the compass set in the cabin roof above the captain's cot, and felt sick.

For four days on the new course the passengers were not allowed on deck except to labour at the pump. With the captain's eye on him, Dand didn't dare speak to them. What good would it have done, anyway? Half of them were ill. Even though the weather moderated slightly, five more died.

At last, from the masthead came the long-awaited cry. 'Land-ho!'

Screams of joy and relief rose from the hold. 'America! America!'

The coast ahead was rugged but inviting under the heavy grey sky, long fingers of white sand thrusting deep among craggy rocks towards green fields and woodland beyond. While the emigrants bundled up their sodden belongings, singing psalms of joy, the captain had the boat hoisted over the side from its place behind the mainmast. In indecent haste the folk were rushed ashore, carried if necessary up the ladder and lowered into the boat, shoved on when they sank to their knees to kiss the sand of their new home.

The minister shouted from the beach, 'God bless you, captain! We are all thanking you—'

'Thank the Lord, sir!' Men were appearing from the far woods. 'All plain sail, Mister Robb. Hoist the boat in later. Up anchor.' Hastily the *Daisy* moved away from the shore.

'Aye, well.' Chuckling, Iain rubbed his nose and grinned at Dand, standing glum by the rail beside him. 'America, eh? God help them. Our turn next. Jamaica, is it?'

'Aye. After a place called Barnstaple for repairs.' Dand's voice was thick with disgust, and he turned away. Iain's casual acceptance and even callous approval of the captain's deed grated on him.

For though Maxwell had been paid to carry the emigrants to Boston, he had dumped them in Ireland, damn his cheating soul to hell. At least they'd know the language. But among the Papists, God help them right enough.

LINK SIX
Gbodi:
Late January, Loko village

P roudly Gbodi fingered her new bead necklace, made
specially for the celebrations tonight. Hers was the
finest! None of her friends had four glass beads and
a whole row of cowries from a place far, far away where
water ran across the ground all year, not just during the
rains.

At the far end of the valley where she normally grazed her
mother's goats, she and her friends were jumping about,
peering eagerly up at her half-brother Omu swaying
perilously in the fork of a high branch. 'Wake up, you
dung-beetle!' Gbodi screeched. 'Can you see them yet?'

'Don't call me a dung-beetle, you monkey! No . . . yes!
Here they come! And they're all there!' Omu scrambled
down, yelping at a thorn-stab, and scampered after his
friends along the path through the head-high elephant grass.

Every couple of years, after the first heavy falls of the
rains, while the women got on with the planting, the older
boys were led away into the bush for two moons for the
training and testing that made them men. Omu, now
twelve, would be in the next group. No child or woman
knew what happened, for the ceremony was a fearsome
magic that no man would betray. Sometimes a boy died,
but not this year; Fola's god baby must be content.

The juju doctor led the group, stroking his thin beard,
smiling and genial as usual today, but still fearsome. Behind
him came the skilled men who had trained the youngsters, a
few of them visitors and teachers from other villages, and
last the new men themselves.

Gbodi gazed in awe at her big half-brother Akin, son of
her father's first wife. No longer a bouncy boy in a flappy
apron, he strode proudly with the men as a man, with a

man's spear in his hand and the scars of male initiation red and raw on his body, face, and arms. The new blue and white kilt wrapped round his hips hung almost to his ankles. Even his eyes were different somehow; colder, distant, not as laughing as before.

Then he glanced down at Gbodi, and she realized that this was mostly acting. The scars hurt; Akin was full of delight and triumph; but a man wouldn't show either. She cheered with the other children, jumping, dancing and somersaulting to lead the group into the village.

It was a great feast. That evening every woman brought to the huge fire her bowls of yams and groundnuts, mealies and sweet potatoes, goat or pig or chicken, to do honour to the new men. The finest kilts or bead aprons and ornaments were paraded. The women danced, and the men danced, brass and copper anklets clashing musically, and they danced and sang together in lines facing each other, displaying their skill and vigour. The young ones giggled about future wives and husbands. Round the edges Gbodi, Omu, and their friends danced, copying and learning, darting among their elders to beg titbits, half drunk on excitement as much as maize beer. Faces flushed dark, oiled skin gleamed with sweat, eyes and laughing teeth flashed white and red—

Behind the huts, a dog tied away from the feast barked a warning. Another.

Men, strangers in white headbands, many, charged out of the dark, brandishing clubs. The village men stumbled to their feet to fight, but their spears were in the huts, and the soldiers drove them back onto the open dancing ground. The women and children fled screaming to hide in the huts, under beds, behind skin stretching frames and water jars. Some dodged or fought through the circle of attackers to escape. An invader snatched a stick from the fire and ran round the outer huts thrusting it into the thatch. In seconds, the village was ringed by light that exposed anyone trying to break away.

Gbodi saw Akin dive out of a hut and stab a man who was hitting the headman. A cracking bang sounded from the dark, with a bright spark of light. Akin screamed, dropped his spear, and fell against the hut wall, holding his belly, blood pouring between his fingers.

Desperately, Gbodi looked round; every space had a white headband in it.

'Here!' Akin gasped by her knee. 'Hide under me. They may think you're dead, like me.'

'You're not!' Gbodi was already squirming under her brother's body.

'Not yet . . . ' Akin gasped again, leaning back to hide her.

The adults and the older children, all those big enough to untie a knot and free the rest, had their hands tied behind them, or, if they struggled, their elbows. They had to sit down in the dancing ground, bruised and bleeding, with ankles tied. Only babies and toddlers were left loose. Sentries stood over them with spears and cudgels, while others, laughing and efficient, went through the huts, pulled out the people hiding there, searched them for knives and added them to the wailing crowd. Everything of value was hauled out: a few bags of salt, beads and cowries, some clothing, spears and knives, skin rugs; not much. Jeering, one man set a brand to the roof of the juju house.

For a while Gbodi thought she had been missed, but two men dragged Akin aside. At his gasp of pain, one examined the wound and then speared him, while the other hauled Gbodi out to join her mother and little sister, a stepmother and uncle, and half the village. The rest had escaped—or were dead.

They lay helpless while their captors celebrated round them, drinking the feast beer, eating the feast food, attacking the women. At length, satisfied and tired, the attackers set a guard, built up the fire with the message drums and thatch from the huts, and went to sleep. Anyone who wailed or moaned was kicked to silence.

51

It was a long, wretched night. Maybe the god had been angered after all . . .

She would not give in! Defying her hollow feeling of impotence Gbodi struggled till her wrists bled. She was tied with leather, not grass rope; the blood softened it, let it stretch, and the slipperiness let her wrench a hand free. As soon as she could move her swollen fingers again she began to work on her ankle bonds, cautiously, not to draw the sentries' eyes.

All night Omu, lying beside her tied too tight to move, watched her in silence and stillness.

Just before dawn the last knot gave way.

Flexing her cramped muscles, ready to flee, Gbodi hesitated. Could she help Omu?

'Go on!' he breathed. 'Take your chance! Go!'

Yes. Cautiously Gbodi glanced round. No one was watching. Fast or slow? Fast.

She drew a deep breath and shot to her feet, already running. Round the nearest hut—a guard in front of her—dodge aside—she tripped on Akin's body, and crashed down. Before she could move, she was seized. She had been free for maybe five seconds.

The leader, wakened early with a hangover, raged at her in his foreign language. Gbodi couldn't understand a word, but everyone understood the spear that he lifted to threaten her.

Behind him, a screech made everyone jump and turn. 'Run, Gbodi!'

During the night someone had sneaked close enough to toss a knife among the prisoners. Gbodi's mother was one of those who had cut her bonds, lying still to let more people free themselves. Now, while about twenty people fled for the forest, Monifa snatched up a long pestle and hit the leader, knocking him into the ashes of the fire.

Gbodi squirmed but couldn't break her captor's grip, as a soldier ran a spear into Monifa's side. She fell screaming, twitched, and lay still.

'Mamma? Mamma!' Mamma couldn't be dead. She couldn't! Not so quickly! Gbodi froze, dumb with shock.

Rubbing his burns, the leader was berating the sentries. The king would be angry, for far too many valuable slaves had escaped already. He didn't intend to waste another. Gbodi was not killed, merely beaten with a whippy hippo-hide rod, retied and shoved back among the crowd.

The prisoners' ankles were freed. Their necks were tied to a strong grass rope, an arm-span apart, four ropes each with seven or eight people. Even the old and crippled were taken. Mothers with babies in arms were allowed to carry them, but toddlers too heavy to carry easily and too small to keep up were driven off. The strangers paid no attention to the women's screaming, but forced them to lift onto their heads bundles of the village's goods, and drove them all forward in a long, jolting, unwieldy line, with a spearman between each rope of prisoners. One man fired the thatch of the remaining huts.

Gbodi's last sight of her home was her little sister, only two years old, standing gazing after them, her thumb in her mouth, while the huts blazed round her.

All day they stumbled along tracks further than Gbodi had ever been before, whipped on whenever they slowed. At noon they reached a village of deserted, burned-out huts. Two women were set to draw water from the well for their captors, and the prisoners were allowed a little too, but after only a few minutes they were forced onwards.

By nightfall, with no food, only that scant mouthful of water, Gbodi was dizzy, fainting, and completely lost. She felt as if she was in a bubble, and cherished it. Outside was unreal. Outside were pain and humiliation, fear and helplessness. Out there, her mother was dead, and her grandfather. Half the villagers were groaning round her, collapsed, too exhausted to move, their aching open wounds clotted with flies like her own. But inside her bubble she was safe. Nothing could get at her, not really, not in here.

The other women, Gbodi's aunts and girl friends, noticed

the girl's apathy and after a few days began to wonder about it. She didn't seem to feel pain or tiredness. Was she in a fetish trance? Was she speaking to the gods? Or just sick? Preoccupied with their own worries about their own families, they avoided her. Only her brother Omu had spirit and kindness enough to trouble with her. He found her whenever they stopped and their hands were freed, bullied her into eating whatever mealie porridge or roasted yams or bananas were handed out, held a leaf cup of water to her lips and persuaded her to drink.

Kept weak and hungry, the villagers tried to plan escape, but the guards knew their trade. They cut forked branches and used red-hot iron rods to burn holes in the forked ends. Then with the rods they fastened the forks round the necks of the strongest, most spirited men, and tied the loose ends together so that the men were held rigidly and painfully apart, unable to move without jerking cruelly at their partners' necks. That stopped any trouble.

Day after day they marched from dawn to sunset, lost in the high elephant grass, their brown skin grey with despair as much as dirt. After the first fast march the soldiers freed their hands in the evenings to let them tend their wounds, but still their cuts and bruises throbbed with pain. Their legs and backs ached. The blisters on their feet and necks burst, filth caked their festering sores, and horse-flies that they could not brush away stung freely. They stopped for half an hour to let a woman give birth, and then were forced on, the women in front and behind her helping her along. Any who could not keep up were left to starve or be killed by hyenas. Once they paused for two days, tied up under guard while the soldiers raided another village. In stronger villages sometimes some of the slaves were sold as casually as dogs or goats, or two sick ones were exchanged for a healthy one who could travel better.

After uncounted days of marching they arrived at a town of high houses with frightening straight walls and corners, and flat roofs instead of thatch. The people here wore cloth wraps from armpit to ankle, or togas of narrow cloth strips stitched together, or wide-sleeved robes, patterned in blue and white, and bright cloth tied round their heads like huge flowers. They looked sleek, happy and rich as they ignored the strings of half-naked slaves being driven past.

To each side of the wide market street was a long thatched hut. Branding irons were produced, and stuck into a brazier of glowing charcoal. Amid a hubbub of screams each prisoner was held still to be branded on the back of the left arm with an Arabic letter. Then they were untied and thrust into the huts, men in one, women and children the other, to cry and comfort each other or slump in despair.

Gbodi sat down, dully leaning against the slatted wall. Ay, luxury, even inside her bubble she felt it, to be able to sit down when she wanted to! She had not screamed; the burn on her arm was outside, far away.

Omu sat beside her, nursing his arm. Dozens of women and children were sitting about, dull and incurious. 'What's wrong with them?' Omu wondered. 'Are they ill?' Gbodi didn't even bother to shrug in response. 'They're not Nupe, or Mossi like us. Maybe Fulani or Yoruba. Those big boys with the face scars are Ashanti. Very fierce, Uncle Mboge says. Perhaps they came this way raiding for slaves and were captured themselves—serve them right!'

He looked at his unresponsive little sister and rubbed his chin in irritation. But she could not help it . . . 'At least I am here to look after you. If I had been a man they'd have put me in the other hut, and what would you have done then?' Gbodi did not answer. He shrugged. 'Ay, what's that?'

The gate opened to let some old women carry in baskets so close-woven they were waterproof, from which they tipped food and water into two troughs of dug-out tree-trunks, like small canoes. 'Come on, I'm starving!' Omu scrambled to his feet and found himself knocked aside.

The Ashanti youths swaggered forward. Arrogantly, they took what they wanted from the troughs, scooping up huge handfuls of the grey mealie porridge till they were satisfied, splashing water over their heads as well as drinking. Only then did they move aside and let the others get near the troughs to squabble for their leavings.

Omu fought to get a couple of handfuls for himself and Gbodi, and a drink of water in a cracked calabash, but some of the younger, weaker children with no mothers to care for them went hungry. 'Why don't we gang up on them?' he muttered resentfully.

'We tried. The guards beat us,' a woman grumbled. 'And so did they. The Ashanti are great warriors. Better leave them alone.'

Days of idleness passed slowly. More people were brought in. The local merchants brought in oil and cloths and even bright jewellery on market days, when buyers came looking for sacrifices to the local gods, or for women to work the fields, but the finery was always collected again afterwards.

Safe in her bubble Gbodi didn't care. She scarcely noticed those who had been bought being led away, crying out to their friends and family left behind. Then one morning she woke up and stretched. She felt—better. Rested, recovered. In touch with the world again.

She sat up, looked round, realized where she was, and suddenly began to gasp desolately.

Omu held her shoulders, steadying her. 'Greetings, little sister!' he murmured. 'Your spirit has returned to you at last.' He shrugged sadly. 'Maybe it was better off where it was.'

Juliet:
January, the Kestrel

O n sailing day Juliet washed her hair straight, hauled it back like Anthony's and tied it with a tidy black bow at the nape of her neck, strapped a stiff calico binder round her chest and dressed as far as drawers and shirt. Her grandmother nodded approval. 'Aye, aye! A fine lad ye make! So far so good, eh? But now it's here, have ye the courage to go on?'

'Yes!' Juliet gritted her teeth. 'I'll not lose my nerve, grandmama, however much you niggle at me!'

'An' what'll ye do if ye're found out?'

That, of course, was the thing she had to face. 'It depends on how papa takes it. But I'd run away as a boy, like your cousin, rather than live here in disgrace!' Juliet laughed nervously. She didn't think it would come to that. She hoped not! 'Look, there's Tony coming.'

'Tell him not to come through. I'm tired, wi' you an' all yer fussin'.' Mrs Smethwick's face softened slightly. 'Go on, then, gel. What ye waitin' for?'

Juliet hesitated, and then knelt by the chair to hug the old lady. 'Thank you, grandmama.'

'Get away, ye soft doxy! Ye'll maybe curse me afore ye're home again. But I suppose I wish ye well. On ye go, ye unnatural besom.' Juliet kissed her, and hurried out.

She missed her grandmother's whisper: 'Come back safe, hinny!'

Terrified and exultant, Juliet opened the door for Tony even as he climbed the outside stair and raised his hand to the brass doorknocker, and dragged him into the passage. 'Get your clothes off!'

Polly, coming from the kitchen to see who was at the door, giggled at Juliet tugging at her brother's waistband.

'Get away, ye saucy baggage!' Juliet snapped, but she was giggling herself, with nerves as much as humour, as she chased the girl out.

Blushing, Tony put on the coat, breeches and waistcoat he had left in a bag, and eyed her, suddenly aware that it was no longer just a plan, it was really happening. 'Are you quite sure . . . ? I shouldn't . . . you shouldn't—'

'Tony! Don't you dare rat on me!' Settling his tricorne hat on her head, she glared till his eyes dropped. 'Good luck with the studies.'

'Good luck with the sailors—and the savages.' Tony's voice was still doubtful, rather resentful.

'Heart up, Tony! Think of being a bishop! And thank you. Goodbye!' Before he could argue any more Juliet hugged him, ignoring his startled jump, opened the door and slipped out and down the stair. Ninny! He wasn't fit to run the firm, not when she could so easily bully him into a daft venture like this. And he'd never make a fuss in public. She was away! She'd prove herself, never fear!

Outside no one moved out of her way, as they always had when she was a girl; to her momentary surprise she was jostled and sworn at for getting in the way of the sailors, porters with yokes or wheelbarrows, stolid or frantic horses hauling carts and sledges among sprawling stacks of barrels, boxes, and bales along the quayside. How freely she could stride out and breathe without her dragging petticoats and tight-laced bodice! She turned, as Tony would have done, and waved up. At her grandmother's window, a thin hand waved back.

'Clear the way, ye sheep-brain blindworm!'

'Mind yer gabby snout, ye hellspawn, or I'll fry yer poxy guts an' feed ye them!' The porter did not even blink, but Juliet chuckled in satisfaction. God bless grandmama!

The *Kestrel* was ready to leave, moored on the outside of the solid mass of shipping three deep alongside the quay. Her mouth dry with nervousness, Juliet followed a dozen sheep and milk goats being led up and down planks laid over the rails of the inner ships. When a goat leaped to escape, clattering back past the cursing sailors, she jumped in front of it and chased it forward again, laughing in excitement. 'Ta, matey!' a man called. Used to Anthony, busy with last-minute work and driving the animals down an almost-vertical ladder to their pen below-decks, the sailors did not give a second glance to the figure huddled in the heavy cloak and hat against the sleet.

Lud, she'd done it!

Get out of sight, to the cabin. The door under the stern decking, Tony said—she hadn't realized it was only raised waist-high. Down three steep steps and keep your head down under the beams, turn left, second door along.

A single door. Drat that useless gowk—

'Losht again, Mishter Shmethwick?' At the irritatingly superior voice she spun round, straightening unwarily. With a vicious crack her forehead met a low beam. 'Mind out, shir!'

Half stunned, staggering and nearly blind, Juliet realized this accident would help disguise any differences from Tony. 'It's . . . it's nothing.' She clutched her head, wiped the trickling blood all over her face and let her voice waver perfectly naturally.

The wizened little man who had startled her puffed scornfully. 'That'sh captain's cabin, Mishter Shmethwick. I'll show ye yours. Again. Besht lie down a while.' He led her back past the steps to the right—drat Tony!—and opened a door.

Luckily, as the owner's son, and the supercargo, Tony had a cabin to himself. She could never have managed if she'd had to share. But lud, this could never be it, surely, scarce bigger than her wardrobe at home? It must be; there was Tony's sea-chest jammed in under a short cot. No window, only light through the passageway door, though a small lantern hung unlit on one wall.

Thanking her helper, she collapsed, curled on Tony's red quilt. Feet stamped above her head. She couldn't stay tamely below, with the adventure just beginning! The blood had stopped, more or less; she wiped her face and headed back up to the deck.

A supercargo was not involved in working the ship. She could stand out of the way in a corner, trying to make sense of the bustle. She knew Captain Owens, fortyish, trim and spare; the towering, red-faced man in the blue jacket must be the first mate, Mister Cartwright; the skinny young would-be dandy with the boils on his neck and the deafening shout would be the second officer, Hunt.

The *Kestrel* was about thirty metres long, with two masts between which two boats were wedged, nested inside each other. Coils of rope, bales and bundles filled the deck. Above, bulky bundles of brown sails were tied up to cross-spars. One long spar was attached at one end to the rear mast at about head-height, with its free end held down by a huge pulley to swing gently just above the big steering wheel. The big gaff or brigsail would be lowered to it from a rather shorter spar high above. Intricate webs of ropes and pulleys criss-crossed between the masts, spars, and bulwarks. She knew some of the words, thanks to grandmama, but the tangle of ropes defeated her. How could anyone find their way through this maze?

Along each bulwark stood a row of six small cannon, with balls as big as a man's fist racked by them. For pirates, or privateers, or the French . . . Oh, lud, she hoped not . . .

She stiffened as her father appeared on the quay to see off his ship. Had Tony confessed, and papa come to haul her away? No; he did not come aboard. Their eyes met. Juliet took off her hat, held it politely across her chest and bowed coldly, as Tony would have done. Would papa recognize her? Apparently not; stiffly Mister Smethwick returned the bow. Was the churning in her stomach disappointment that he didn't know his own daughter, or exultation at her escape?

'Upper mainsail and jib.' The captain's voice was calm. With no other orders, none of the shouting and confusion she had expected, sailors trotted up spidery rope ladders to drop a smallish square sail high on the mainmast and hoist a triangular one over the bows. 'Cast off.' Men jumped to and from the ship alongside, freeing ropes.

Mister Smethwick took his hat off to salute the ship as the crowd cheered and waved. Juliet hesitated. Papa was doing what he thought was right. And she wouldn't see him again for maybe a year—maybe never . . . She waved her hat. Her father's grim face broke into a smile, and he waved back; tears pricked her nose, but her heart felt warmer. She'd prove her determination and ability, even to him!

Daintily the *Kestrel* moved out towards the open sea, threading delicately to and fro through the crowd of ships, barges, boats of all sizes both anchored and moving. Beside the wheel, the captain indicated each change of course with no more than a calm word, while Cartwright and Hunt bellowed at the crew to haul round the sails as needed to catch the wind, and at smaller boats to stay clear.

'Set the gaff, Mister Cartwright. We have room now.' A huge square sail was lowered to the stern spar and hauled out to one side. As the sea swell began to heave the deck gently beneath her feet, Juliet exulted silently. She was away! She had done it!

'Head better, Mishter Shmethwick?'

Lud, that was her—and she knew the lisp. 'Yes, sir, thank you.' Where was he?

'Don't call me "shir", Mishter Smethwick, shir. Just Bert.' The shrivelled old man was hanging in the rigging above her head, grinning gummily. 'I'm a boy.'

Did he say he was a boy? Balding, toothless, he looked a shrunken, if spry, eighty! 'You . . . er . . . you've been at sea for a long time, Bert?'

'Five year, shir. Shince I were eight.'

'Eight?' Lud, he was only thirteen—three years younger than herself! 'Wasn't that young?'

'Aye, shir, but I'll be rated sheaman next year, an' able sheaman 'fore I'm shixteen, no question!'

'Well done! Captain Owens must know he can rely on you, Bert.'

Bert beamed gummy approval. 'Great man, the cap'n! Don't believe in floggin', Mishter Shmethwick, can ye credit it? On a shlaver? Looks after us, shee? He's a damned—' he glanced guiltily towards the captain '—good physh—physish—dammit—doctor. College trained, shee? I'd still have me teef wi' 'im.' He grinned up at her. 'Losht 'em two year back, on the *Good Venture*. Shcurvy.'

'Sh—scurvy? What . . . er . . . ?'

'Get it on long voyages. Boils all over, an' ye weaken, an' yer gums rots an' yer teef falls out. Cap'n puts lime juish in the rum. Yugh!' His face distorted in disgust. 'Shpoils the drink, but shtops the shcurvy. An' 'e feeds us well, an' we got 'ammocks 'stead o' lyin' on deck.' Bert nodded emphasis to his next words. ''E don't need to get 'is men from the Baltic Fleet!'

'Er . . . why would anybody need to hire Danes?'

'Danes? Oh, ye means Scowegians!' The boy cackled. 'Baltic Fleet's a tavern, shir! Most 'Pool cap'ns 'as to buy a crew from crimps, kidnappers, shee, wot drugs men in their gin, or knocks 'em out an' carts 'em aboard. 'Pool cap'ns don't pay as well as Lunnon or Bristol, shee? But Cap'n Owens do. I gets three shillin' a week, an' 'e don't cheat ush. Sho we stay wi' 'im, even if 'e don't 'old wi' swearin'. Religioush, shee?' Juliet nodded; her father always said a captain who didn't pray was bound to be unlucky.

From behind Juliet a voice snapped, 'Boy? What are ye at, damn yer eyes?'

'Mister Cartwright . . . ' At Captain Owens's quiet voice the first officer's big open face flushed even redder.

'Bosun told me to frap them flyin' pennants, shir!' Bert chirped.

'About time. The ship looks like a French laundry! Get on with it an' stop lallygaggin'!' As Bert industriously wrapped twine round the offensive loose ends of rope, Cartwright glowered down at Juliet. 'Bumped yer head, Mister

Smethwick? An' no mama to bandage it? Ye should practise humility, sir, keep yer head low aboard ship!'

'Yes, sir.' Juliet flushed in her turn. Was he normally this bad-tempered? Or had Tony put people's backs up? At a tongue-click above her, she glanced up; Bert gave her a wink.

Feeling suddenly more cheerful, she glanced astern and noticed a fast-moving little ship scudding after the *Kestrel*. Above her, Bert followed her gaze. 'Hell an' damnation! Shir! Shir! Navy cutter, shir, port quarter!'

'Thank you, boy.'

Juliet jumped at a sharp crack. 'That was a gun! Is it firing at us? Why?' she hissed.

'Gonner shink ush! Shwim for yer life!' Bert's face filled with alarm—fake alarm, Juliet realized with relief and some annoyance; he was teasing her!

'It's the signal to heave to. Acknowledge, Mister Cartwright, and comply,' Captain Owens said, looking grim. 'Dock the lookouts a day's rum for inattention, Mr Hunt, and the boy two for swearing and playing the fool.'

Bert, busily tying off his twine, pulled down the corners of his mouth.

The *Kestrel*'s head turned up-wind. Her decks were abruptly deserted apart from a handful of men slackening ropes, so that the sails flapped uselessly while the smaller naval vessel drew near, tossed a rope across and bumped to rest alongside.

Bert had vanished.

Captain Owens tapped Juliet's shoulder. 'Hold yourself silent and do not interfere, Mister Smethwick.' His eye was cold and disapproving. 'Your father's purse has no influence here.'

Tony had clearly annoyed everyone! Nervously, Juliet edged up beside the second officer and murmured, 'Would you be kind enough to explain, Mister Hunt?'

'Demned press-gang!' Hunt scowled at an officer, even younger than his own twenty or so years, nimbly jumping across the bulwarks. 'The Royal Navy's always short of men, Mister Smethwick, with these French wars. So they have licence to impress men, snatch 'em off the demned streets. Off merchant ships, too. If they decide to take you, sir . . . ' He shrugged, then smirked. 'Unlikely, though, sir, I assure you, seein' as who you are!'

The lieutenant lined up the visible crew for inspection, while his tough-looking men searched below decks. 'Don't sailors want to serve their country?' Juliet whispered. 'Are they afraid of battle?'

'Hah! They'd have no demned trouble if it was just givin' the Frogs pepper. Be an inducement, sir, rot me if it wouldn't! Ever been on a navy ship, sir? Treat the men like dogs. Worse, God rot me. Captain Owens runs a tidy ship, but some naval captains are . . . ' he shook his head '. . . demned lunatical, sir. Order two, three dozen lashes, for a tar drip the size of your toenail on the deck or a smear on their brass-work, or not movin' smart enough, or any demned reason. Starve the men, drive 'em to death, inspect 'em every demned hour day an' night—who's to stop 'em? Demned little gold-braided gods. Need demned marine soldiers aboard to enforce order! Our men can skip in any port if they ain't happy. Lose their pay, o' course, but what can ye do? But not navy crews. They mostly don't set foot on shore in England, in wartime. Kept aboard under guard, or locked up in demned prison hulks like convicts.'

He flourished a grubby handkerchief, glancing sideways to check that she noticed the lace trim, and blew his nose noisily. 'Deserters are flogged round the fleet.'

Juliet was perplexed. 'Round the fleet? Sir?'

'Rowed in a boat round the harbour after court-martial, an' a hundred lashes beside every demned ship in harbour. Could be fifty. Worse than hangin'. Cripples 'em. Mostly die, o' course. Not demned surprisin', eh?' He shook his head in pretended sympathy at her shock.

To Juliet's astonishment, the navy men were laughing and joking, exchanging gossip and cheerful insults with a few of the *Kestrel*'s hands over the bulwarks; how could they, with a life like that? 'So our men are hiding.' She wished she could.

'Like demned woodworm. Some of 'em are old navy hands. The bluejacket'll hunt 'em out, God rot him, plenty of experience, an' if he can't find anybody he'll demned well pick some.' Below decks wood splintered, to a shout of triumph. Hunt shrugged. 'That's one caught.'

'Can't Captain Owens stop him? Just say no?'

'Proper fire-eater, ain't you, Mister Smethwick?' Hunt chuckled in admiration. 'Prevent a king's officer carryin' out his duty? Demned treason, sir! Hang you for it, rot me if they wouldn't! Captain Owens buys letters o' protection from the demned Admiralty, but it don't always work. So he takes on a few bad bargains—poor seamen—that he can cheerfully sacrifice if he has to.'

For twenty minutes the *Kestrel*'s officers fumed while the lieutenant and his men searched. Three men were found, four offered, and three more simply picked out. Shouting, one struggled until he was stunned with a cudgel and heaved over the bulwarks. One elderly man sobbed; the others climbed across in resignation, one even joking. A woman hurried up with bags of clothes, tossed them to the cutter's deck and clambered sullenly after them. 'McKay's wife. He's a sailmaker, that's why they took him. Demned bad luck—only woman aboard, so who'll look after the youngsters now?'

Juliet's jaw dropped. She had not realized there would be a woman on board, who might have recognized her as female. She was sorry for Mrs McKay, but she was glad the woman was gone. A mean, nasty, shameful thought.

The lieutenant mounted the ladder to the poop. Juliet froze. Did he want her?

He stopped in front of the hostile group and lifted his shabby cocked hat to them. 'My regrets, gentlemen, but duty's demands . . . ' He looked directly at Juliet, with clear distaste. 'Mister Smethwick?' Her heart quailed. 'Last week, sir, we opened a cask of beef supplied by your father to feed the men who fight for him, sir, who risk their lives and ruin their health so that he may live and trade in freedom under British rule, not French tyranny. The cask, sir, was full of horses' heads. When you next write to him, pray present him with our respects, and say we trust that his profits are satisfactory.' Not waiting for a reply—not that Juliet could have given one—he turned away in disgust.

Captain Owens was speaking almost before the lieutenant had left the deck. 'All plain sail, Mister Cartwright. Course east by south and a point east. Let us avoid any other vultures.'

'Aye, sir.' Glad to be away, the sailors were already clambering up the tracery of rigging as the mate's orders snapped out. Mister Hunt moved off to the mast of which he was in charge.

Her knees suddenly trembling with reaction, Juliet watched as huge sheets of canvas were dropped or raised and hauled to the proper angle to the wind. She felt sick.

Did her father really do that? Sell horse heads instead of good salt beef? He couldn't know . . . or could he?

He would, if it made a profit.

'Sails set and drawing, sir,' the mate reported.

'Thirty-two minutes, Mister Cartwright. We can do better than that.'

Cartwright jerked his head towards the naval cutter approaching the next ship leaving the port. 'Best not show them we have more men than they thought, sir.'

'Quite right, Mister Cartwright. We only lost ten—better than I feared. The rest may come out now.'

Juliet jumped. At the word a panel popped open beside her knee, and from what looked like a solid block of wood too small to hold a pair of boots Bert squirmed free. Grinning, he eased his neck, knocked the panel back in place, pulled his scabby forelock to the captain, and jumped down the ladder to the main deck.

Captain Owens was smiling. 'Resourceful, the British

seaman, eh, Mister Smethwick?' He looked sympathetically at her disturbed face. 'You are not responsible for your father's actions, young man. But it is as well to be aware of them, so that you may, if you are so minded, improve upon them when you can.'

'Yes, sir.' Gratefully, Juliet nodded. 'I will do so. I swear I will!'

'That, Mister Smethwick, is an oath to which I have no objection.' With a slight smile the captain turned back to watch the sails.

LINK EIGHT
Hassan and Gbodi:
February

T imbuktu was a weary shadow of its greatness two centuries before, when it rivalled Venice for wealth, art, and learning. Wars had destroyed its heart. The libraries and palaces were in ruins, their yellow mud-brick walls melting, sand sifting over their mosaic and marble floors. It was still a trading centre for the salt brought south from the desert mines, but its schools and gardens were gone, and prices were high. Uzum hired new paddlers to take the boats on to Gao, and they left as quickly as they could.

Three days later a slave died, painfully, from a poisoned arrow fired from overhanging trees. The guards shot their muskets blindly into the leaves while everyone else paddled away, hard.

Next day the oldest and biggest canoe ran up across a submerged tree-trunk and snapped in half. No one drowned, and most of the goods were salvaged, but four sacks of salt melted and a chest of glassware vanished in the ooze though Hassan and the other good swimmers dived for it until they were exhausted.

'We've no room for slaves now with only three boats,' Hassan complained. He had joined his father under the canopy of the middle boat—not that he was scared of poisoned arrows, of course.

'We have to give goods to buy the slaves, don't forget, and we can buy another canoe. Also, only Allah the Merciful knows the hour of every man's death, but perhaps half of us will die before we return.' Uzum shrugged as Hassan gasped. 'Did you not realize? For those who return, the rewards are high. And no one thinks it is his turn to enter Paradise this trip!'

The next day Bozo, their chief guard, broke his leg. Uzum paid the chief of the nearest village a bag of salt to care for him, but as he told Hassan, 'Bozo's musket is a temptation as well as a defence. The chief may kill him for it. Allah the All-Merciful knows it's all I can do; Bozo is in His hands now.'

Then the cook disguised rotten fish with spices, and they all fell ill with dysentery. Vomiting violently and passing blood, doubled up with pain, Hassan groaned, 'May a thousand devils each give that dog of a cook a thousand times these pains! Allah forgive me for cursing!'

They had to stop for six days, eating nothing, until the disease worked itself through them. Four men died and several deserted, including, not surprisingly, the cook. Nine others were so weak and dispirited that they had to be sent home. Luckily a trader heading north agreed to take them, pick up Bozo too, and carry them all as far as Timbuktu, where they could find a boat going home.

The paddlers said someone had cursed the voyage, and demanded that Uzum should sacrifice one of the slaves to break the spell. When he refused, most of them ran off.

'Should we turn back?' Uzum wondered, but Hassan urged, 'You would lose respect! All my friends—all our friends would laugh at us!' He forced himself to his feet. 'See, I am recovered! I can help you! You must go on! We must!'

'Certainly God loves the steadfast.' Uzum felt discouraged, but his son's spirit and determination heartened him. He shrugged, unwilling to disappoint the lad. '*Ya Allah*, I've survived worse. We'll go on.'

He set Hassan to bargain with the local headman to hire new boatmen. 'Two bags of salt each? Too much—one bag. Very well, three bags between two men.' The chief would probably take one of the three, as his cut. 'And dash for your help, a cooking pot of brass, shining like the sun! And you will dash us a goat and ten chickens.' Uzum nodded approval. 'Giving presents' was more polite than trading.

Just before Gao they unpacked their best gowns, long and white with bright patterns printed and embroidered on breast and sleeves, and their embroidered skull-caps. 'We must make a good impression,' Uzum warned Hassan. 'We must show that we are important men, due respect.'

The lookout in the bows of the lead boat beat a drum to announce their arrival, clearing a way through a shoal of fishing canoes to the landing beach. The chief's herald rode down to welcome them, on a spirited black horse with a carved and tasselled leather saddle. He himself was no less gorgeous in a red coat with brass buttons. 'From the white men!' Uzum whispered to Hassan.

The houses here were like Hassan's home but smaller, and yellow, not cream. Thick buttresses held up the walls, the corners had spires of mud brickwork like ox-horns painted white or blood-red, and curves and patterns were carved and painted round decorated black doors. The streets were worse, though; as well as the usual stinking open drains, full of ducks and dead dogs, they had holes big enough to drown in where mud was dug during the rains to build and repair the houses.

Gao, Hassan knew, was a centre for the slave trade for many tribes. When the local kings went to war, the victors brought their prisoners here to sell. Other slaves were debtors sold to pay their debts, or surplus children sold by their families in a bad year, or mad or crippled, criminals or for any reason not wanted by their villages; sometimes simply people of outlying villages, attacked by their own chief's soldiers to train his army and buy his luxuries.

A crowd of women came out into the wide courtyard in front of the palace to greet them. Chasing away dogs, donkeys, and giggling children, they offered cool water and beer, bitter cola nuts which made you feel tipsy when you chewed them, and sweet oil to soothe the skin. Hassan had seen unveiled women in Djenne, of course, his own family, slaves or pagans in the market, or the Tuareg whose men were veiled, not their women, but to be surrounded by laughing women

70

commenting freely and boldly about him, nodding and flirting, was shocking. With some embarrassment he edged away from two pretty girls rubbing scented shoulders against him.

'Friendly, aren't they?' Uzum grinned. 'The chief here is an old man. His wives are bored, and glad of visitors.' He chuckled at his son's horrified face.

'They are all his wives?' There were a hundred of them, at least!

'Or slaves, or concubines, or daughters. I'm not going to ask! The king at Oyo, to the south, has six hundred wives, poor man. He is a pagan, of course. His eldest son has to kill himself on his father's grave, to stop all the sons fighting about who will be Crown Prince—I wonder how they pick the next king afterwards. Relax, boy!'

Suddenly, with a blast of horns and drums, the heavy door opened. Everyone fell to their faces. Two senior wives helped the chief hobble out. He was indeed ancient, with robes of thickly embroidered blue cotton, and a straggly white beard. He sank into his carved, cushioned chair with a grunt of relief and set his bare feet on a richly beaded stool. A slave held a wide red umbrella to shade him. Stools were brought; the guests sat in front, his counsellors in a semi-circle behind him.

The herald interpreted Uzum's respectful greeting, the chief's reply and two hours of polite chat about the difficulties of river travel; boats as opposed to camels, mules or women for carrying goods—horses, of course, were for riding only; the chief's new horse; hunting, and the weather, and other light subjects to relax the visitors. To one side musicians played quietly, flute, konting, and kora, and small hand drums. Hassan kept his eyes firmly down. Those young wives were smiling at him again—disgraceful—he must stop blushing!

At last the chief asked, 'What great reason has brought you here, my friends?'

Uzum gestured for their slaves to bring forward the

71

presents: a carved chest made of sweetly scented sandalwood, five lengths of brilliant silks from the north, and a purse of silver coins. They inspired a long speech of welcome. Clearly, the old man was telling his counsellors to treat these generous merchants well. Hassan saw his father wince; he had given too much, and prices would go up to take advantage of his wealth!

That night a feast was held for the newcomers. For the first time in his life Hassan drank corn beer, not realizing how strong it was, and had to be carried to bed.

Next day, as they walked from the house they had been given to the slave huts, he had trouble opening his eyes. Heartlessly his father laughed at him. 'Stick to cola nuts in future.'

Hassan sniffed. 'You seemed to be enjoying it, whatever the Prophet said, blessings and peace be upon Him.'

'I had to be polite. Learn, my son, that this is the real world of men, not your school. Certainly many things happen out here of which the imams disapprove!' Uzum smiled up at his tall son, and nodded to the guard to open the men's hut. 'Come along. It's time for some work, after our lazy trip!'

Hassan had often been to the dusty open market in Djenne, but the low roof and bamboo walls here half suffocated him. Ignoring the stink Uzum looked round. Eighty or so men were lying and squatting, tied to long chains down the centre of the hut, watching him warily. 'I want about two dozen men in all, and a dozen women and youngsters, but we can buy more further south. Let's see that big fellow first.' He beckoned; the man stumbled to his feet.

The other traders were picking their own first choices. One after another, the men in the hut were examined, their teeth and eyes, their feet and hands, every inch of their skin. Scars were probed and poked, to check that they were thoroughly healed. What skills did they have—blacksmith, weaver, farmer, horseman, musician? Language did not matter; whatever their tribe, the slaves would have to learn the speech of their future owners anyway.

For four hours, Hassan listened fascinated to his father explaining the less obvious points, good and bad. 'They've been cleaned and dressed up for us. Ignore the clothes and beads, and look under the oil and paint for sores. Avoid any with signs of disease, or a crippled limb. That one's mad, those too old. No, not that coughing one, nor the limping Fulani, look at the old brand on his face, the ridges on his soles. He's been a slave for years, and a bad one, to be bastinadoed so badly. Mark this Wolof with the bright eyes. He's young and clever, or he'd not be fat, not in here! He'll be dear, but worth it.' Uzum's thumb pushed up the next man's lip. 'Look, rotten teeth. That doesn't matter for the salt mines, they never last two years there anyway, but white men will want better. This tall Yoruba looks dull, but I think it's just despair. His hands are horny, he's a good worker. Mark him, too. This Zarma's tongue has been freshly slit, maybe yesterday when we arrived, to hide an ulcer underneath, see? This one is better—thin, but wiry and tough . . . '

Two men wore heavy wooden collars, rubbing sores on their shoulders. Others had wooden blocks as fetters. Uzum warned his partners against them. 'Ashantis, captured when they came raiding north here. Very fierce and difficult to control. They say the white men like them, but I'll not risk it, with so many of our own guards gone.'

By the time they left to pray, and rest out of the midday heat, Uzum and his partners had put their paint marks on fifty-three men who interested them. For some days they would bargain, fiercely polite, until maybe half were bought.

Despite the heat, Hassan couldn't rest. 'Father, can I try? On my own?'

Tugging off his skull-cap, lavishly scratching his scalp, Uzum fell on his rope and canvas bed. '*Ya Allah*, that's better!' He yawned. 'Very well. Pick me out some youngsters in the other hut, and when it's cooler I'll come and see how good your judgement is.'

Proudly Hassan marched down the street and gestured to the guard to open the other shed. As they walked in he almost fell over a boy and girl, squatting on their heels behind the gate playing woaley in holes in the sand. He kicked the playing stones aside in annoyance.

About thirty youngsters and half as many women were sitting around. Hassan pointed to a big, sturdy boy and beckoned. 'You, come here!'

He had neither the experience to recognize a young Ashanti, nor the natural authority of his father. The youth sat still.

Hassan blinked at the defiance, and then beckoned again, brusquely.

The boy sneered up at him, and scornfully turned his back.

Hassan found his hands and jaw were trembling in frustration. He had never felt so helpless. All his life he had been treated with consideration, the youngest, the favourite, indulged and obeyed by his mother and sisters as every boy was, praised and admired by his friends and teachers; only Taranah scolded him badly. Being mocked made him feel weak and ridiculously inadequate, which first dismayed and then infuriated him.

The guard's hippo-hide rod made the boy stand up, but it wasn't the same.

The child who had been playing woaley was grinning. A girl! How dare she? Angrily, Hassan snatched the whippy rod. He slashed at the girl, who clutched at her chest, screaming, over-acting—everyone knew wild blacks didn't feel pain like civilized people. He raised the rod to strike again, and found it torn from his grasp and himself jostled so roughly that he fell headlong.

All round, there was a gasp of astonishment—and satisfaction. The girl seemed most shocked. 'Omu!' she cried, scolding anxiously in her own language. 'Omu!'

Hassan rose slowly, trembling with rage, brushing down his robe. He was not hurt except in his precious dignity. His father would lose respect because of him.

His attacker tossed the rod aside and stared defiantly.

Hassan picked up the rod and advanced on the boy who had dared to strike him. 'I'll beat you!' he snarled. 'Beat you till you bleed!'

In Barnstaple Iain worked away happily with the carpenter and the workers of the small shipyard. He never thought of running away. Dand thought of it constantly.

Captain Maxwell was no fool, though. Before they entered the harbour Dand's ankles were linked with an arm's length of chain. He could work, but couldn't move silently enough or fast enough to escape. No one cared; criminals were commonly chained, and runaway or unruly apprentices and schoolboys were often fettered for a while to teach them manners. Dand was even glad of it, for, oddly, while he was chained Maxwell beat him less. It was sickening, though, to see green land over the bulwarks but not be able to slip away.

Maxwell worked as hard as anyone, twelve hours a day sweating in spite of the cold. However, he still found time to go out socially. Every evening, as soon as it was too dark to see, he washed his face and hands, put on his coat and went ashore, to return drunkenly happy—at first. After a few days he began returning equally drunken, but sour.

One evening, on his way out, he jerked his head to Dand. 'Come wi' me, loon.'

Surprised and pleased, Dand clinked down the gangplank. Right enough, it was dod's mercy Maxwell hadn't reeled into the harbour already. A run ashore to help him home was a grand treat.

The tavern they entered was full of the roar of drunken, boisterous voices pierced by yapping and a high, thin squealing. Jolly red faces crowded at long tables polished by decades of spilled beer, raised round a fenced pit about four metres across. Clearly the men and doxies of the town came here for cock- and dog-fights, badger-baiting or, as tonight, ratting, betting on their terriers killing sackfuls of big brown rats poured into the pit.

Dand grinned; ratting was grand fun.

'Drop it—dead 'un! Sic 'em, Fury!' The crowd was yelling, jumping with excitement, cheering on two small dogs that were snapping and snarling, ignoring the rats' vicious bites, shaking them to break their backs, dropping them instantly to dive for the next. The women screamed and clutched at their escorts in fake alarm as agile rats leapt desperately up the walls of the pit to fall back to the sawdust and the hysterically happy terriers.

'Eight to Fury,' the pitmaster was calling the score. 'Fourteen to Minerva—fifteen—and the last to Fury. Sir Michael's Minerva wins, fifteen to nine. First kill to Minerva, in nine seconds, kill-out in two minutes sixteen seconds. A champion little bitch, sir! Hope that bite on her eye heals fast! Pay out, Albert! Drink up, gentlemen!'

The handlers lifted out their squirming dogs and a boy jumped down to clear away the bodies, while the old bet-holder handed out the stakes he had held, never mistaken about odds, a shilling or a face, and the potboys carried round trays of alemugs.

Maxwell pushed forward through the crush to speak to the pitmaster, who frowned. However, when Maxwell insisted, he nodded and rang a bell for the attention of the roistering crowd. 'A novelty for ye, gentlemen. Tonight Captain Maxwell here hopes to repair his bad luck over the past week. He offers as a stake not a horse or a dog but this slave boy, Dandy, about fourteen years old, healthy and willing, trained as a cabin boy or house servant, worth thirty-five pounds. He wagers at evens against the next dog, Parson Carruthers's untried pup Dasher, killing one dozen in under four minutes. Those wishing to place a bet may examine the lad.'

Dand's heart jumped and twisted in dismay. Slave boy— not even indentured! As a bet! No! What could he do? Tell them he was free? Who would believe him? Run or fight? No chance. Beg—no, never that! That man there with the religious collar, would he not object? No, he was leaning back laughing. Two men were coming over to feel his muscles and check his teeth. Damn Maxwell! Maybe a new master would be kinder. But any change was frightening when you were helpless. And he'd never see Iain again—after losing his family, and everything . . . Damn them all!

Six times Maxwell won his bet.

The last match was not a dog, but a man. Yan had been a soldier, so famous as a prizefighter that his colonel had set up a match between him and a champion from the navy. The two men had slugged it out for four hours through sixty-two rounds, until Yan was crippled and battered unconscious. He was left where he had fallen; his colonel would have flogged him for losing the match, and his sergeant kindly 'forgot' him. Now, Yan was a huge, shambling halfwit who survived by begging and raking in middens, and occasionally earned drink and a shilling by fighting rats with only his teeth, his hands tied behind him. His shaggy beard protected his mis-mended jaw, and two glasses of gin had him too drunk to care about bites anyway. Scrabbling, roaring, and biting, he shook the last rat to death in less time than Dand had been bet against, grinning and spitting bloodily under the cheers.

Maxwell slapped Dand's shoulder. 'Aye, loon, ye've brought me luck. Ye've won me two hundred pound!' Dand felt oddly proud that he was worth so much. 'Now I can pay the repairs!' His money worries over, he was jovial and relaxed again, and tossed Dand a coin.

A groat? Fourpence? Ach well, better than a kick. The potboy, eying Dand's chain with sympathy, brought him a bowl of kitchen scraps and a quart of ale for a penny. In greasy contentment he squatted by the fire to eat and doze in the warmth while Maxwell caroused with his friends.

Kicked awake, he helped the captain back to the ship willingly. 'Luck—ye're a lucky loon!' Maxwell mumbled over and over. 'Ye know who that was? That I was talkin' wi'? That was two men.'

'Aye, sir, Ah noticed.' Dand shoved his master upright again.

Maxwell was too happy to notice the dryness of Dand's tone. 'Two . . . two men. A judge an' a squire—that's a laird, loon. An' they've a cargo. Was on a ship as was wrecked. So they asked would I take it to trade. Damme, it's ten years since I went for black cattle. Twelve. They said they liked a man as would take a risk—because I risked you, loon! So. They'll supply the trade goods, an' I'll supply the ship, at half shares in the profit. An' next year I'll go wi' a cargo o' my own. An' then I'll be rich! Rich! Slaves— that's where the silver is . . . Silver? Gold! Ye've brought me luck. Rich . . . '

Dand supported him up the gangplank, down the steps and into his bed. Slaves? Ach well, it couldn't be as bad as those filthy, starving Highlanders.

For two more weeks they laboured. When the repairs were done, they jammed the hold with stacks of blue and checked Guinea cloth and made clothes, muskets and gunpowder, rum, glass beads and cowries, and fancy goods—old armour, mirrors, trumpets and cymbals, shoes, hats and bonnets, china plates, tools, tin and brassware, whatever might tempt an African's whim.

The dawn they set sail again, six blind-drunk men were delivered by the crimps, dropped into the rope locker to be brought up next day blinking and vomiting, and driven to work. One actually fought, screaming, 'You can't do this to a gentleman!' Maxwell, himself suffering from a hangover, had the man tied up and slung under the bowsprit, dangling soaked and frozen for twelve hours. He was half-dead when hauled back aboard. There was no more trouble.

As they sailed south, in the stormy Bay of Biscay they overtook a ship limping along with a damaged mast. 'British flag,' Maxwell declared. 'We'll see if she needs aid. It's our Christian duty. Mister Robb, have the men ready to load the guns fast; she could be a Frog, foxin' to trap us. Or a pirate. Terrible, the pirates, Dandy loon! But it pays, aye, it pays well. An' easier work than slavin'. Any ship can attack ye—or be attacked . . . ' His smile was sly.

The *Vixen*'s captain refused their offer in a strong Devon burr; clearly no Frenchman. 'Kind of you, sir, but we'll fetch Gibraltar for repairs without assistance.' Red-coated marine soldiers were drilling ostentatiously on the main deck, ready to repel attack.

Dand almost laughed at Maxwell's wistful sigh as he waved to Robb to relax and put on more sail, and raised his hat in farewell. Serve the rogue right! But maybe . . . The *Vixen* was about eighty metres behind them, and going slowly. If he slipped down the stern unseen, and let the *Daisy* sail away from him, he could easy swim across . . .

Peuch! What a stink was blowing from the other ship! Dand screwed up his face. He knew that reek; he had smelled something near as bad for six weeks from the emigrants.

He jumped as Maxwell tapped him on the head with the trumpet. 'Forget it, loon.' The thin man smiled, not unkindly. 'Ye'd never reach her—there's tiger fish in the water here. Sharks. An' even if ye did, ye'd be no better off. Ye'll no' nose a stench like that till we fill up wi' slaves. For she's a prison transport, loon. If ye stole a shillin' or a spoon, an' weren't hanged, ye'd get sentenced to ten years' hard labour in Sydney. That's in Australia. A boil on the arse-end o' creation.'

'The town or the country, sir?' Mister Robb asked.

Maxwell barked a laugh with no humour. 'Both.'

'Have you been there, sir?'

'Once.' Maxwell grimaced. 'I've never seen filth an' cruelty like it, never. No' even in the coal-mines. A stinkin', wretched hell-hole, run by the redcoats on rum an' floggin'—an' they order lashes no' by the dozen, like Christians, but by the hundred! The prisoners, them that live to get there, they're sold off to the free settlers as bound labour an' no' let come home even if they survive, an' few o' them do. And,' getting back to the main point, he waved a finger at Dand, 'if ye did get aboard her, ye'd join them. Now put by the hailer, Dandy loon, an' be glad ye're here!'

Running to obey, Dand shivered. If even Maxwell condemned Australia's brutality, he was glad to have been stopped!

A fine westerly trade wind carried them smoothly past Portugal and Morocco, well out from the coast. 'There's a many ships goes missin' hereabouts every year,' Maxwell observed. 'There's reefs an' shoals ye can't see for the mists an' the sand in the water. We'll stay well clear, an' keep the lookouts alert for pirates, an' Sallee galleys, unless ye're wishin' to be a Moorish slave, eh, Dand?' He chuckled at Dand's shock. 'An' Portugoosies as go far east, right to the Bight o' Benin or Angola. They can stand the heat better than white men. They've great factories there, barracoons wi' thousands o' slaves to take to Brazil, an' they're no' shy to ram a rival on their way. As if there wasn't black ivory enough for all o' us!'

The air grew warm, and then suddenly hot. The captain, one of the few who kept on their shirts, after three days offered, 'A mug o' rum to the man can peel the biggest strip off his hide!' Dand had been running round even more naked than the rest of the crew, his never-before-uncovered skin turning crimson and baggy grey with blisters. With Iain's help on the back bits he stripped himself, elbows to neck to knees, and triumphantly spread out on the deck a ragged, holey, but undoubtedly single sheet. They shared the prize; it was worth the pain of the sunburn.

Maxwell was delighted when only six weeks after leaving Barnstaple they sighted two small hills on the far coastline. An odd scent wafted across the water, hot and musky, full of rotting leaves and smoke and spices. 'Cape Verde. Ahh, smell that, Dandy boy!' He sniffed luxuriously. 'The stink of Africa! I first sailed here wi' my father, twenty years ago. God, it's good to be back!'

'Do blackies live in houses, like people, or make nests in trees?' Dand wondered that evening. He was sitting with Iain, stitching at new breeches he was making of canvas from an old sail. 'Do they walk on their feet, or go on all fours like animals until they're trained? Have they hoofs? Ah know they don't wear breeks, but what have they for the kirk on the Sabbath? Do they have a proper language, or do they just grunt, like? Will we get ashore, d'ye think?'

'Ashore?' Iain sniffed. 'Dafties ging ashore. Snakes an' scorpions an' creepy-crawlies as lays eggs under yer skin, an' the maggots eats ye alive. An' the bad air gives ye malaria or break-bone fever. An' the savages eats ye if they catches ye. You stay where ye're safe, ye gowk. We'll get more nor enough o' the stinkin' blacks when we get 'em aboard.'

'Dozy dummy!' Chuckling, Dand gazed over at the distant shore in the last light of an immense crimson sun. What marvels the world held! 'Dod, I can scarce wait!'

For days they sailed along the immense coast. 'No smokes—that's odd,' Maxwell commented. 'Ye'll often see the savages signallin' to ships that they've slaves to sell. Aye, well. We'll run in and see what Betsy Heard has at Bereira. Her da was a Liverpool man that set up a slave tradin' post there, an' took a black wife. He sent his daughter home to be educated, but she came back and took over when he retired. So now the mulatto bitch is queen o' the river. She has fine blacks, Mandinkos from up-river, clean an' clever, better nor Efik or Fantis.'

As they worked into the river mouth Dand gazed at the shore, at the strange trees growing right down into the sea, at the rolling green of the forest, at the long thin canoes dashing out through the surf to meet the ship, at the low buildings huddled above the tide mark. He was eager to see this Betsy; would it be her top or bottom half that was white?

However, he was not taken ashore. Maxwell told him, 'Betsy may come visitin' for a wee jaunt. Unwrap a cake from the locker, an' some cheese, three bottles o' claret an' the good glasses—well polished, Dandy! An' if ye nibble I'll skin ye!'

Dand was sullenly picking some currants off one of the captain's heavy fruit cakes, stored in waxed paper in the cellaret built under the cabin floor, when he heard laughter on deck. Giggles. Women's voices! He ran out to see.

The deck was full of colour and laughter, crowded with dark brown people. The women were wrapped in bright cloth, some shockingly bare above the waist; the men wore worn breeches or loincloths or even nothing at all, like the children. They were offering the crew strange fruits and nuts, a frothy white beer, brilliant, squawking birds and little furry babies, straw hats, carved ivory and seashells. Everybody was happy; even while Mister Robb was shouting at boys climbing the rigging, he was laughing with a half-naked woman in each arm, their red mouths and pink palms bright against the dark skin.

'Aberdeen was never like this, eh?' From a corner by the galley Iain waved, ripping one brown-spotted spike off a huge bunch. 'Ah got all this for just the one rusty nail! Here, try it—sweet an' soft—like my wee black bird here!' He cuddled the giggling girl clinging round his neck. 'Na, ye eat the innards, no the skin, ye gowk!'

Cautiously Dand nibbled. A musty, sweetish taste and an odd mushy texture—but after three months at sea, it was delicious. What could he steal, to buy some for himself?

For an hour he roamed in a glow of wonder amid the happy crowd, staring at the women, playing with the babies. A sailor told him they were called monkeys; the fur must rub off as they grew, for in a sling on a woman's back was a bigger baby that looked normally smooth, though dark brown, of course. He scratched a little boy's skin to see if the colour came off, until the child yelped and jerked free. These folk smelled different from the sailors, or the Highlanders. And they laughed constantly—that was different, too.

Then he chanced to glance over the side. A canoe was approaching, bearing a familiar glower. 'Mister Robb, sir! Here's the captain—an' in a right temper!'

As Maxwell climbed the rope ladder, his anger was incandescent. 'Cripples an' dotards! Ninety-eight ships in the last month—there's no' a nigger left on the coast!' He glared round; these blacks were free traders, but could he grab them anyway, even if it made him unpopular with other captains? No. Warily, they were already slipping away, the children diving straight over the side among the thronging canoes. 'Set fore an' main, an' up anchor, Mister Robb! There's five hundred factories along the coast, Cape Coast Castle, Apollonia, Cape Mount, Tres Puntas, Montzerado, Whydah, Calabar, Bonny—a thousand! And twice that o' chiefs wi' slaves to sell. I'll get my cargo, if I have to go to Madagascar!'

Gbodi and Hassan:
February—March

H assan felt excited and pleased with himself. He had upheld the authority and dignity of his father and himself. That would show the savages! They jumped now when he beckoned them, even the boy who had ignored him before; very satisfying. Very.

Though there was a look in their eyes . . . Fear, and resentment.

They couldn't do anything about it! He was master!

Silently, Gbodi cursed him. Omu had only been trying to save her when she had done nothing. She knelt by him, fanned him with a palm leaf, and glowered at the bully.

From nowhere, his teacher's voice floated into Hassan's mind. 'If you see an injustice . . . ' And slaves should be treated kindly . . .

Nonsense. This wasn't an injustice. Savages must never get away with insolence, let alone a blow. Not in the real world.

When Uzum and the rest of the group turned up later in the afternoon, Hassan had picked out three boys and a girl. 'Good choices!' Uzum complimented him on three, but dismissed one boy. 'No, not that one. He's an Ashanti.'

Hassan bit his lip. If it hadn't been for this boy upsetting him . . . He glanced over at the smaller boy he had beaten, curled in the corner . . . Maybe he should not have been so violent . . . But all takes place as Allah wills.

Like his partners, Uzum ignored the hurt boy. Anyone wild enough to deserve so severe a whipping, and now needing nursing, was a bad buy.

However, one of the men, Ali, called out the little girl kneeling beside the boy.

Her heart pounding, Gbodi had to come forward. Rough

fingers forced her jaws apart, made her bend over, poked and prodded her all over. Cold eyes examined her eyes without seeing her as a person, and moved coldly on to her ears, her neck, the weal across her chest. 'What happened here?'

The guard played down the incident. 'She was cheeky—the young master there taught her a lesson!' When Ali nodded approval without enquiring further, Hassan felt rather relieved.

Shaking with humiliation and fear Gbodi found a red thumb-print being pressed on her forehead. A sacrifice mark! She rubbed it off. Instantly the hippo-hide rod welted her thighs. Yelping, she suffered the mark to be repainted, and this time left it alone.

When she was dismissed she squatted again beside Omu. 'They'll buy me—I know they will! What shall I do without you? I'll die. I know I'll die. They'll eat me! That woman over there said—'

'She was just trying to scare you. They wouldn't eat you, you're too thin,' Omu scolded, to calm and comfort her. 'They want you to work, not to eat.' He hoped. He had heard the rumours too. Who knew what foreigners did? He licked his lips. 'I'm dry!'

Ali noted the child bring her friend a calabash of water. Helpful and willing, he thought; her value rose a fraction.

'Now listen.' Omu moved unwarily, and winced. Ay, he felt so old! 'Remember old Uncle Mboge? He was taken as a slave when he was very young, but after some years he managed to escape and get back home. He said if you learn fast and behave well, don't argue, keep smiling even when you feel bad, try to please, then masters treat you kindly. We can pray for that, anyway.'

'Will our gods be with us, so far away from home?'

'Of course!' He hoped he sounded more certain than he felt. 'And we can fight back! Learn whatever you can, and use it to fight them.'

Gbodi nodded vigorously. 'That boy, the one who had you beaten—I'll never forgive him.'

'Fight all of them, in every way you can. And be like Mboge, try to escape. Even if you die trying, anything that hurts the slavers is worth it!'

Over the next few days the haggling went on. Hassan admired the way his father could bring the asking price down and down. 'I fear ten brass pots and two swords is more than I would get for that man. Allah comfort the poor soul, what a pity the bonesetter could not set his arm quite straight! What did he do to be punished so—to be thrown against the ceiling a dozen times? Happily there are many other markets down-river. Alas, I could not pay more than two pots and a bag of salt. I can add this perfume bottle, in respect for you . . . That boy, for the red saddle? *Ya Allah*, a good jest! Look at the workmanship—the finest leather, the rich embroidery— and smell the scented oils! I expect three healthy women for it alone. Well, to please you, I might accept two and a girl—or three young men . . . '

He was polite and cool at first, then gradually keener and keener until finally a bargain was struck at maybe half the original price. In public he shook his head sadly, lamenting, 'You are so clever, so expert—I cannot match you! At this price I must make a loss, my master will rage at me, but what can I do? In your hands I am soft as the clay from which Allah formed Adam!'

In private that evening, though, relaxing on his bed, he chortled, 'From what I learn, I'll get ten times this price from the white men. That will pay all the expenses and leave a fat profit.'

'Uncle Farouk will be pleased.' Hassan opened the shutters to let in some cool air before the mosquitoes came out, and poured a cup of water for his father.

Uzum nodded thoughtfully. 'Yes. I wonder—should I set up on my own?'

Hassan jumped. 'Yes, father! Please! You are important

enough—you could become rich working for yourself, not for him!'

Only heathens and prisoners of war could be kept as slaves. Since Hassan and his father were True Believers they were free, though in fact it made little difference to the way they were treated. However, his grandmother was a slave. The Koran said that when a slave girl bore a child to her master, she should be freed, and her child too, though of course his grandmother could not go home, she was too far away, and also Farouk never released anything he had in his grip. Chuckling, Uzum had often told him, 'Farouk is very like our father, who could squeeze a lump of butter the size of your head out of three date stones, the miserable old goat!'

The respect due to the child of a slave, though, and that owed to a rich trader, were very different. Uzum eyed his son's eager face, but shook his head and shrugged. 'Would it be worth it? I could then keep all my profit, but Farouk's name carries weight from here to Algiers. Certainly it is a protection for me to work for him, and in a hundred towns I can buy goods simply on his name. Would people trust me alone in the same way? There are good and bad points. I shall consider it.'

'Oh, do it, father! Then I should be an imam, and rich as well!' Hassan's heart beat painfully at the hope. Praise and gratitude to Allah the Compassionate, the Gracious! In the meantime he grinned at his father. 'I can help more. Let me captain the new boat for you, father,' he urged. 'I know how.'

'From your wide experience?' Uzum laughed, but considered it. 'Ach, why not? As long as you stay right behind me. Yes, I think we'll do that.'

'We.' Hassan's heart glowed at the compliment. He was a partner now!

Four days later all the bargaining was finished. Gbodi, though she did not know it, had cost a length of striped silk with a flaw in the centre, and six strings of cowries. The merchants packed their unused goods and a few elephant and hippo teeth, and unpacked their personal branding irons, while the guards lit the brazier by the hut door. The slaves were brought out, their hands tied in front of them to a link rope, and branded a second time with their new owner's mark. When Uzum saw Hassan wincing at the screams, he shook his head. 'It only hurts briefly, my son. It marks each man's property, and identifies them if they escape. And besides, having our mark on them makes them feel they are part of our group, part of the family.'

Gbodi could have told him that was nonsense, but she was sobbing too bitterly. She felt this burn, but worse was her heartbreak at being separated from Omu. Only three men and a woman from her village were in the coffle. Her world was gone. Like the rest, she wailed and moaned.

'Move them along! Down to the river!' Uzum called.

'Fight back!' Omu yelled through the bamboo wall of the hut. Over the mourning cries, Gbodi heard his voice. It only strengthened her despair.

She had been brought into Gao from the landward side; at first sight of the river she gasped at the wide brown flow. Water really did run over the land! But when her rope of slaves was pushed down the bank towards a hollow log that floated on the water, she screamed and struggled until one of the guards half-stunned her, picked her up and dropped her into the canoe, gashing her leg on the side.

Whimpering, she was pushed forward tight against one man's back, crammed in by the knees of another huddling up behind her, while they rocked and wobbled appallingly close to the water. The young bully urged his men to cram in more and more, until an older man stopped him. A few were moved out to another canoe, but she had still no space to move.

The bully climbed in, with more men, some carrying flat wooden spears which they dipped in the water; the townsfolk shoved the canoe off the bank, and to Gbodi's terror they moved away from the land. Screeching in hysterical panic she lurched up, her linked neighbours joined her, the canoe overturned, and they were all in the river.

Luckily the water was still shallow. Coughing and spluttering, dragging Gbodi and the other women tied to their rope, the men floundered towards the shore, where the townsfolk were rolling about the bank, slapping their thighs, helpless with laughter.

Hassan was not laughing as he waded ashore. He had paid Gbodi too little attention to recognize her, but he felt angry that again his authority had been damaged.

Quickly, despite the hilarity, the canoe was righted and the unsold goods fished out. The slaves were beaten and reloaded. Sore and defeated, they crouched unmoving as the canoe started out for the second time.

By evening their muscles were locked with cramp. Gbodi could not stand, let alone walk, but was kicked till she staggered with the rest to a pen.

Slowly, day by day, the river grew wider, till Gbodi could see only one bank at a time. In many places the spiky roots and trunks of mangrove trees heavy with leaves and vines advanced in dark aisles right down into the water, unlike the scrubby thorns Gbodi was used to. Strange birds honked and screamed among the branches. Vast banks of reeds filled every silted shallow till the voyagers often had to wade behind the canoes, long strings of slaves and guards all splodging and stumbling for hours through the rustling, towering stems. Their feet, softened and cut by the roots, stirred up a choking stink of rot. Leeches clung to them like huge black slugs. Floating weeds hid crocodiles sliding hopefully among them. A dying girl, bitten by a snake, was thrown overboard; before they were out of sight she was dragged under.

At last the islands that had dotted the river grew so many, splitting the river up into so many channels, and the current became so slow that it was impossible to tell which was the right path. The guides demanded more pay; reluctant but not surprised, Uzum had to agree.

Day after day they travelled on. Most towns along the Niger welcomed slavers. On one island there was even a vast market whose merchants boasted they sold eleven thousand slaves a year. Local slaves, who might try to escape, were cheap; those from a distance fetched high prices. Two of Uzum's companions sold up at a good profit, bought cheaper slaves and left for home. Ali, however, decided to go on with Uzum and two canoes to see the sea.

Huge horse-like heads, half submerged, gazed at them from open pools where hippos wallowed during the stifling heat of the day. One man chewed through the neck rope and dived over the side; he was wounded by a guard's musket, and then bitten in half by a hippo disturbed and enraged, perhaps wounded, by the shot. Gbodi sat impassive, but Hassan was scared when the hippo surged towards his canoe, its vast teeth still dripping red. The guards all fired. Bellowing, it sank and swam away.

'*Ya Allah*, a pity,' Uzum called into the scared silence. 'No roast hippo steaks tonight!' Hassan led the laugh to hide their relief, each guard boasted that he had fired the shot that drove off the monster, and the slaves learned that trying to escape was dangerous for many reasons.

Every day huge blue flies blanketed everyone, drinking their sweat, choking eyes and mouths and noses, biting, stinging. The near-naked slaves suffered appalling lumps and sores from the poisoned bites. Every night swarms of mosquitoes attacked. Many of the party fell ill with the shakes and fevers of malaria. Several slaves died, to Hassan's annoyance.

Ali picked Gbodi, as the smallest and least dangerous of his purchases, to be untied to kneel behind him in the canoe and at meals, to fan him and drive off the insects.

Smile, Omu had said. Smile, obey them, please them, and fight back . . . Gbodi smiled. She fanned willingly, obviously did her best to understand and learn, eagerly ran errands, was submissive and helpful, until no one paid attention to her.

She could not sing, dance, or drum to call her gods, but during the slavers' prayers one evening she found a chameleon, the gods' messenger.

Its rolling, independent eyes, and the way it could change colour, terrified her, but she forced herself to pick it up respectfully. She did not die; the gods were pleased with her. Anointing the little reptile with a sacrifice of blood from a thorn-prick, she whispered to it. 'Carry my words! Yemaya Okute, goddess of the river, great fighter, curse them! Curse them! Let their bellies rot! Let them swell and burst! Curse them to death! Help me fight them!' Then she dropped the chameleon in the fire.

Suddenly the gods sent her an idea. She picked up a handful of shit, added some pus squeezed from her mosquito bites and dropped the mixture into the slavers' stewpot, stirring it to hide what she was doing. She began to do it every night.

Four days later Ali and four guards fell ill, and died.

Beneath Gbodi's calm face her heart burned in fierce triumph. Her gods were with her.

Twenty-five others fell ill; six slaves died. A pity, but worth it. The bully's turn soon . . .

J uliet gazed round in satisfaction at the brilliance of the water and the sky, the bustle that she was beginning to understand, the faces she was beginning to know. She had done it! In spite of a dozen frights and near-discoveries, in spite of rats and cold and wet and the constant creaking and groaning of the ship, and food that would have sickened even little Polly, she was coping well. Far better than Tony would have done!

For a couple of weeks, ignorant of men's behaviour among themselves, she had accepted Hunt's flattery and loutish charm at face value. Then she had overheard Bert and another boy, acting a play. Bert had bowed deeply, hands flourishing in a perfect imitation of Hunt's extravagant gestures, smarming outrageously. 'Dear Mishter Shmethwick, pray gimme yer opinion o' thish shnuff! Though 'tish not the quality ash wot you is accustomed to!'

His mate smirked modestly, in stomach-churning mimicry of Juliet herself. 'Mister Hunt, I fear I am no expert!'

'Nonshensh, my dear shir! If I may shay sho! Yer natural tashte is better nor mosht men'sh ekshpret—ekishper—dammit—ye know a demned lot about it! About everythin', rot me if ye don't! Yer daddy'll gimme a ship, won't 'e, if I licks yer bum enough?'

Blushing deeply, Juliet had slipped away before they saw her, and treated Hunt's crawling more coldly. A week later, as she dodged yet another attempt to curry favour, she noticed Bert winking to his mates. Had he put on the little play specially for her to see? Cheeky little devil! But after a minute's anger she realized he had given her advice, as he couldn't have done openly. And at least he seemed to have no idea that she wasn't a lad. No one did. She had done it! Grandmama would be proud of her!

Today she was standing by the bulwarks in shirt sleeves. The cotton of her chest binder was surprisingly cool in the pleasant heat. In a sunny corner behind her Bert was milking the nanny goats. Only fifty metres away on the sand of Gran Canary a dozen sailors were enjoying the novelty of a bonfire to boil a cauldron of vinegar, to scald out the casks before refilling them from a clear stream. She sneezed at the drifting fumes.

Behind her Captain Owens laughed. 'Pungent indeed, Mister Smethwick! But we need at least fifteen thousand gallons of clean water, about seventy tons. You remember the *Zong*?'

'As everyone must, sir.' Juliet eased her shoulders in distaste. 'A hundred and thirty-six ailing blacks tossed overboard to claim the insurance. The captain should have been tried for murder, not fraud, and certainly not acquitted. It seems to me quite wrong for the judges to say he was no more to be blamed than if he had killed sick horses.'

'I agree, sir. An appalling waste.' That wasn't exactly what Juliet had meant, but no one interrupted the captain. 'Quite unnecessary and mainly due to lack of water. In Africa's heat, sir, water turns green and foul in days. You must scour out your casks and fill them clean at the last possible moment, to increase your chance of the bounty.'

'Bounty, sir? Might I ask . . . ?'

'Most ships lose a quarter of their cargo on the voyage. Many lose a half. However, if only three in a hundred die, the government awards the ship's surgeon one hundred pounds. In six voyages I have earned it four times.' Owens looked justifiably proud. 'Good food and water is vital. And lime juice for the crew.'

For once, Juliet could show competence. 'To prevent scurvy, sir.'

'Indeed.' Owens was surprised. 'It is only recently recommended.'

Give credit where it was due. 'Bert told me of it, sir. He is most helpful.'

'Good, good. He is your ship's daddy, eh?' Owens smiled at her perplexed face. 'Someone who helps a newcomer, a landsman, learn his way about a ship.'

'Er . . . yes, sir.' It pleased her that the captain looked as approving of her as of the boy. 'Would you be so kind as to advise me also, sir? My lists mention manillas. I understood that was a kind of rope?'

'Manillas are C-shaped rods of metal with knobbed ends, in all sizes from finger rings up to anklets.' Owens smiled slightly. 'You might call large iron ones the pounds of Africa, copper or brass ones the smaller coins, and cowries the pence.'

'Cowries? You do mean the sea-shells, sir? Really?'

'Indeed. Reasonably light, durable and impossible to counterfeit—ideal coinage. We have twenty crates of them, as well as our other goods, to buy up to three hundred and fifty slaves.'

Juliet did not see how so many people could fit aboard, let alone be kept healthy, but he must know what he was doing. 'I understand we also seek ivory and gold, beeswax and spices, sir?'

'And dyes and hardwoods.' Owens nodded approval. 'Your attitude has vastly improved since we sailed, Mister Smethwick. You seem eager to learn, more attentive, more capable.'

Juliet bit her lip modestly. 'At my sister's urging, sir.' Tongue firmly in cheek she added, 'Juliet is practical, intelligent, and efficient—a most unusual girl.'

'Indeed?' Owens approved. 'I shall hope to meet her on our return.'

'She will be delighted to make your acquaintance, sir.' Encouraged by his good humour, she decided to ask a question that had been worrying her. 'Sir, I believe many

Nonconformists condemn slavery as inhuman and degrading to both slave and master. My mother has several abolitionist friends. The movement is growing, even in Liverpool, since Prime Minister Pitt spoke in its support—though he has stopped now, since the French revolutionaries abolished slavery. No one wishes to be linked with them! But some hold that Christian baptism to save the souls of the Africans justifies—'

'A minor factor, sir. Though Christian surroundings, even on a plantation, instead of the savagery and warfare of their native jungles, can only benefit the blacks.' Owens's lips tightened in disdain. 'Sceptics like the Jacobins, atheists and deists—of whom I fear Pitt is one, and also that idiot Wilberforce—denounce slavery, certainly. So do some Nonconformists; the Quakers keep no slaves, and the Methodist preacher Wesley urged his followers to free theirs, though few obeyed him—the Methodists and Baptists own thousands of blacks. But should true Christians oppose it? Neither Christ himself, nor any of the early Christian writers, ever condemned slavery. Many urge the humane treatment of slaves, certainly, but the early church leader Augustine in his famous work "The City of God" flatly declares that slavery is the Lord's punishment for sin, and in God's eyes slave-dealing is no crime.'

He considered, staring out towards the shore. 'The blacks taken as slaves seem luckless, but might well die of disease or war, or be sacrificed to their heathen gods, if they were not removed from Africa. You dislike the cruelty and injustice of slavery, as all good men do; but you are predisposed to softness. You are rich, and, if you will forgive me, pampered. My mother died of starvation on our farm in Glamorgan, when I was six years old.' Juliet's jaw dropped in shock. 'Life is cruel and unfair for whites, as for blacks.'

To hide his emotion, apparently, Owens sent a glare down at the launch ferrying back the full casks. 'Mister Cartwright, I have no wish to remain here until next year!' he called, before turning back to Juliet to continue his lecture.

'You must also consider the purely practical argument. Without slavery the New World plantations and their trade in sugar, rice, and tobacco, and nowadays cotton, which provide a huge part of Britain's wealth, simply could not survive. Half the small manufacturers of England, who supply goods for the trade, would be ruined. The fight against the French would collapse for lack of taxes. Thus even if the abolitionists could persuade Parliament to ban the traffic, the Africa trade must necessarily continue. No, no. Man will learn to fly before the barren places of the earth can become fertile farmland without slaves.'

He nodded seriously. 'Also, while the trade is legal, the Government may monitor it and soften its harshness, as with the bounty, and laws regulating the number of slaves that may be carried in ships of different sizes. Decent men like myself take care of our blacks, making an honest profit from a vital and respectable, if unpleasant, trade. I treat my cargo with as much care and consideration as is consistent with safety. And, of course, profit. There are far worse ships than mine. Many, I fear. Even most. However, if the trade is outlawed, its conditions can only worsen. None but rogues will take part in it, smuggling slaves, cramming in as many souls as they can without regard to their humanity.'

'Souls, sir? Humanity, sir? Niggers, sir?' Mister Hunt, just within earshot below them on the main deck, was supervising the men hoisting the full casks aboard and lowering them back into the hold. He looked up in protest. 'Half animal they are, rot 'em, more than half!'

'They are human beings, sir,' the captain reproved him.

Hunt was undaunted. 'Humans don't live like pigs, sir! Skins like leather, don't feel pain. Bare naked an' shameless as animals, men an' women——'

'For the heat, sir?' Juliet suggested. Samson and Pompey weren't animals . . .

'Must disagree, sir! Regretfully!' Hunt smirked. 'Nig-nogs are stupid, vicious, untrustworthy brutes! Even the dem—er—the abolitionists won't have 'em in their societies! Help

97

'em, like feedin' stray cats, but don't want to cuddle 'em, an' who's to blame 'em? Dem—er—cannibals! Cowardly too, rot me if they ain't! A white man'd die before he'd be a slave!'

Juliet noticed a wry expression on the captain's face. 'You do not agree, sir?'

'That all slaves are cowards and morons? Scarcely. You know Bob Bigtooth, our linguist?' Juliet nodded; Bob was one of the dozen black sailors. 'He interprets for us among the new slaves, who may be of twenty tribes all speaking different tongues. Bob speaks at least eleven of them—scarcely a sign of stupidity, Mister Hunt? Then, the Muslim janissaries were among the fiercest fighting men ever known. In their heyday no European army could stand against them, and they were slaves, black and white, fighting side by side. Besides, it is estimated that there are over ten thousand white slaves in North Africa.' As Hunt's face flushed, the captain added grimly, 'Ten years ago I was captured by Sallee pirates, and myself enslaved for three years till I was ransomed. A vile experience, physically and mentally. Starvation, theft, humiliation, beatings. No slave aboard my ship suffers as I did, if he behaves well.'

He frowned down at the flabbergasted officer. 'Mister Hunt, shall I send for your men's hammocks so they may snooze more comfortably?' Scarlet, Hunt turned to urge on the work.

Juliet puffed in satisfaction. A harsh and disagreeable task, but necessary, and done as kindly as possible; exactly how she had seen the trade. And Owens seemed to bear no hatred towards his former captors. He was a rational man, and a good Christian. The abolitionists had always seemed cold and joyless, with no real kindliness or humanity—no wonder her father refused to have them in the house. Yes, they were wrong.

While she thought about it—'Sir, in my lists I found crates marked Slave Ironware. What—?'

'Chains, restraints of various kinds. You should check them, see for yourself.'

'Yes, sir.' She mustn't fool herself that the trade was gentle; you had to face facts, even if you didn't like them.

The *Kestrel*'s lowest deck, little more than a metre high, just above the keel, was packed with half a year's stores; dried beans, rice, flour, candles, iron-hard ship's bread, cheeses, casks of salted beef, rum, beer, and water. The main hold above it, where as Juliet knew you could only stand upright between the beams, held the animals' bad-weather pens and also the trading merchandise, packed tight with only narrow passages left between the wedged stacks of goods.

'Thish way, shir.' Bert, who had appointed himself Juliet's guide, took one of the lanterns he had filled with oil that morning, and led her edging through the maze, ducking automatically now under the beams jammed between the temporary bulkheads to hold all steady. 'Black's a chimbley in 'ere, innit?'

'More like an oven now!' Juliet panted, wiping her forehead with her wrist, and squeezed between bales of cloth. 'How would you know? Ever been up a chimney?'

'Gonner be shweep, wun't I?' With no teeth to shine, Bert's face was indistinct in the dim light, but his tone told her he was grinning. 'Master shweep, wi' a fightin' bull-terrier an' a knobby shtick—grand, eh? Ain't thish them, shir?'

Eleven crates with the marks of five different small iron-foundries. Right. She attacked the top lid with a crowbar. 'What sh—stopped you? Soot up your nose?'

'Neh! Keep yer 'ead down an' yer gob shut—same as ev'rywhere, eh? Go up a chimbley shtill roastin' 'ot, I could! An' wriggle up tight bits. Five pound ol' Warby paid foundlin' 'ospital for me, 'cos I were shmall,' he boasted. 'Jilly, me mate, she got shtuck. 'Ad to break down chimbley wall in an old geezer's bedroom to get 'er out. Took 'em two days. Cor, ol' Warby were ragin'!' He cackled with glee.

'She wasn't dead, was she?' Jammed in a black smother, so near light and safety—oh, lud!

Bert snorted in contempt. ' 'Course she were! Pity—she were a good 'un.' He shrugged, dismissing his friend's death as just an unpleasant fact of life.

Tugging, Juliet panted, 'Why did you leave?'

'Ol' Warby rubbed 'ot salt in me busted blisters, to toughen me elbers an' knees. Ow, it 'urt, lor' lumme din' it just! Put some weight on that, shir, yer finickin' about like a girl! 'Ere, give over, lemme do it.'

'Go on, then!' The irony didn't even register as Juliet waved him on. 'So you ran away?'

'Woon't you?' The lad heaved till the nails splintered. 'Got it! Go ahead, shir!' Levering off the lid, Bert hopped up to perch on a convenient barrel. 'Tried street-sweepin', brushin' 'orse-shit off crossin's for ladies, but local lads drove me off. Din't fancy fact'ry work—good pay, sixpence fer fifteen hour, but neh! An' thievin's dangerous.'

'You didn't fancy being hanged or transported? Understandable—'

'Neh.' He grinned. 'Local prigs woulda knifed me. An' beggars is worser. Sho I stowed away, shee, an' look at me! Able sheaman in five year!'

Juliet was investigating the crate, clinking and clattering. Bert commented from his three trips' experience. 'Shmall shtuff. Neck rings. Them below's got shpikes for bad 'uns.' She found a bag marked 'SPECULUM ORIS—4'. 'Hey, know wot them is, eh? Betcher don't!'

She shook her head blankly at the sturdy two-pronged iron forks, as big as her fist with fore and little fingers straight, the points bent up in a curve. 'Toasting forks?'

'That's a good 'un!' Bert guffawed till he nearly fell off his barrel. 'Fer feedin' niggers. Them as won't eat. Can't 'ave 'em die an' cheat their owners, eh? Sho ye shticks points in among 'is teeth, shee, an' levers 'em open, shee?' He demonstrated. 'Breaks 'is teeth if 'e shtruggles. An' then ye pours in shoup, shee, an' 'olds 'is nose, an' 'e gotter drink or drown! Good, eh?'

'Good?' Juliet found she could scarcely breathe. All possible care and consideration . . .

Mustn't be squeamish, like a silly girl. It was necessary— and it must be right, if papa did it.

Like selling horses' heads for beef . . .

The trade winds gave them week after week of glorious, exhilarating sailing, rigging humming musically, white sails towering under hot blue skies. To pass the time, the captain painted water-colours; Cartwright made delicate silk lace, his huge hands deft among the bobbins; Hunt wrote long-winded poetry, often asking Juliet's approval, which taught her self-control. The sailors held dancing classes, developing their hornpipe, and embroidered their shirts and trousers with bright silk.

Juliet wanted to go skylarking in the rigging with the other youngsters, but the first time she tried to climb the wobbling rope ratlines, she froze at head-height above the deck.

'Come on, shir!' Bert encouraged her, dangling above her. ' 'S easy!'

Her brain knew that she was safe, of course she was, the men raced about the ropes like monkeys . . . But she couldn't! To her furious humiliation, she simply could not make herself unclasp a hand or lift a foot to move either up or down.

Suddenly a ferocious bellow bayed at her heels. 'Get up there, ye yellow rat! Now!' A rope-end stung her breeches. Terrified, she bolted up the ropes, to cling gasping to the mast. On deck, ten metres below her, Mr Cartwright was grinning up at her. 'Didn't think ye could, did ye?' he boomed. 'Ye'll make a man yet!'

Bert and the whole crew were watching, laughing, some cheering. Juliet hung on, beginning to breathe again. She had done it! She could do it! At last she could grin back, and even wave. But how did she get down?

With grim determination.

She snipped off short Hunt's, 'Hit you, sir! Shocking! Your father will—'

'My father, sir, would be grateful to Mr Cartwright, as I am. For the valuable lesson that in an emergency I can find the strength to do what I must do, more than I thought possible.'

Grandmama would approve.

Nevertheless, though Juliet forced herself to clamber about the rigging occasionally, she was never at ease there. She knew she could if she had to; that was enough.

From a ship from Brazil they bought several bales of cheap cigars and ankers of gerebita, a strong, rough brandy. Owens smiled at Juliet's raised eyebrow. 'Blacks, like sailors, demand strong liquor. We must oblige them, however we disapprove.'

Was that hypocrisy, she wondered, or common sense?

Brazil, it seemed, took more than half the slaves captured, though mostly from Portuguese traders. The West Indies and the American plantations were always eager to buy slaves. The problem might be finding any to sell. Twice they paused to speak to west-bound slave ships. These disturbed Juliet; they stank like stables, and a ceaseless moaning almost drowned the captains' voices answering Owens's questions about the black markets.

'The guns we sell encourage the kings to make war, as is their nature in any case. Then they sell us their prisoners. This year, though,' Owens complained, 'there is an outbreak of peace and a glut of traders.' Along the sandy African coast were scattered towns with fields and orchards, their anchorages crowded with ships, but always they passed on. 'We'll head on east, to the Bight itself. There's a man there who has helped me before. The blacks there are Yoruba or Ibo, or Efik, mostly farmers who work well, though they are rebellious and tend to kill themselves if not treated kindly.'

Kindly? Like with the horrible iron mouth opener? Juliet winced.

At last they dropped anchor. Across two miles of breaking waves, this beach looked no different to Juliet from any other they had passed, merely a few huts on the sand under palm trees, but Owens ordered, 'Mister Smethwick, break out a big gilt mirror, some rolls of blue Guinea cloth, a bale of cigars, a sack of cowries. Open an anker of gerebita.'

Less than an hour afterwards a dozen natives shoved a canoe down the beach. Juliet, breathless with excitement at the bulwarks, admired their skill as the canoe leapt over and through the huge surf that could so easily swamp it; they weren't cowards, nor half animal, even if they did wear only a cloth round their hips.

A dark brown man climbed aboard. Tall and elegant, grinning wide, he wore a red checked shirt and blue breeches, torn but decent, and to her amazement emptied a pint mug full of gerebita in one long swallow without even blinking. It would have killed her!

When he was introduced to her, he proudly showed an armlet carved from a slice of tusk. Burned on it with a hot nail were the words 'JIM SCARFACE SNOW BLUEBELL A GOOD MAN'. After a minute, she realized that he was speaking in English; 'Jim Scarface, me! See!' He pointed to a deep gouge across the bridge of his nose. 'Machete cut. Slabe fight, Jim help *Bluebell* cap'n. Him say good man, Jim Scarface! Gimme token for show udder ship. Good man, Jim! You dash Jim now.'

'Good man, Jim! We dash you plenty!' Captain Owens assured him, offering the gifts Juliet had hunted out. 'You help us now. We need four hundred slaves. You get 'em?'

The black man nodded, beaming. 'Get plenty slabe, cap'n, good cabiceer, Jim! No man not get slabe good like Jim! King man him come small time, you dash plenty plenty, Jim get you good slabe!'

'Good man! You'll see us right!' Another pint of gerebita followed the first, and Jim swung down into his canoe, waving cheerfully as he left.

'A king man, sir? And where should we dash?' Juliet asked as they waved back.

'The local king's representative will arrive as soon as he hears of our presence, to collect his master's tax for permission to trade, and to demand dash; presents, Mister Smethwick, bribes, the universal and shameless custom here. Dash oils the wheels of the trade, for the cabiceers—the shore traders, that is, like Jim—for the king and his official, for everyone. Think of it as an unofficial but essential sales tax.'

'Sir?' Juliet hesitated, biting her lip. 'Jim's words are simple, but . . . '

Owens smiled. 'But you feel that he is not? Well done, Mister Smethwick! Hunt sees in him merely a higher form of monkey. Remember, Jim knows more of English than you do of his tongue. He has to be clever, to deal as successfully as he does with powerful strangers, both European and the tribes inland. His smiles disarm our hostility, but could conceal his own. He understands more than he speaks, and his speech, I believe, is more simple than it need be, to make us feel superior and therefore less cautious. He helps us, we make him rich. But given a chance, Mister Smethwick, Jim will cheat us as readily as any dockside trickster selling fake gold watches to sailors for five shillings. Be wary—always be wary!'

E ast the *Daisy* sailed, and further east, peering
doubtfully in increasing frustration at each town
and river crowded with exasperated ships, the
gunner's daughter well exercised, right across the Bight of
Benin and on south. At last she worked her way cautiously
up a sluggish river, the only ship there, to tie up to a jetty
made of three rotting tree-trunks, at one end of the
anchorage of Loanda, in the kingdom of Angola. 'God send
us slaves here!' Maxwell prayed.

Huts swarmed along the twisting, rutted lanes, though
some of the houses further inland were large, with deep
verandahs shaded by palm-leaf blinds, thatched with huge
flat leaves, and guarded by high, spiky wooden fences. Dand
found it startling that every face was dark. Everyone in the
languid bustle that greeted them, porters, boatmen, donkey
and mule drivers, the swarming children and hawkers, all
had dark brown skin. It made the place feel—odd. Uneasy.
Outlandish—well, what else? He chuckled, hugging himself
in delight.

Most people were dressed in blue and white patterned
cloth wraps, with huge, bright, exuberant turbans; those in
European dress were dull in comparison, the women's lace
frills grey, unstarched and limp. There were no white
women.

As black men jumped to tie the last rope, a bright yellow
open carriage drawn by two white mules lurched through
the throng. The passenger was not a black man, but not
white either, Dand thought. Blue-black of short hair and
yellow of skin, the elderly stranger lounging on the seat wore
an earring, a big ruby in his right ear. His open-necked
cream silk shirt was sashed with a fringed scarf patterned in

brilliant blues and reds, over loose white breeches, bare calves, and embroidered heel-less slippers. Outlandish again. Where Maxwell was already itching with sweat-rash, fully and formally dressed in woollen vest and drawers, linen shirt and neckcloth, waistcoat and coat, cocked hat, black stockings and buckled shoes, just as in Aberdeen, this man looked cool and comfortable.

He leaned forward to beckon Maxwell with a palm-leaf fan. 'Senhor Lopez, Ruiz Lopez, at your service, sir captain. You seek slaves? Ah, you have good luck. War is begun again, and new coffles are come down-river this day. I run biggest barracoons in Loanda. I see you right with king. Come to my house, sir captain, drink, be welcome! I give you a beautiful girl, or a boy if you prefer, and we discuss business later, no?'

A boy? Dand shivered. That was something Maxwell hadn't tried. Not that Dand could have done anything about it if he had. A couple of the sailors had offered, but he had managed to get out of it with a joke. But this man seemed to take it for granted.

All ready to follow Maxwell ashore, Dand was again told, 'Set foot on shore, loon, an' I'll skin ye.' Dod! Aye, well; with a villain like Lopez about, maybe he wasn't too disappointed.

Dand enjoyed the town. Discipline relaxed considerably, for Maxwell stayed ashore in Lopez's house, paying taxes and dash, picking slaves, gambling at night. Girls and hawkers came freely aboard—Mister Robb cursed them for stealing anything not nailed down, and much that was. Dand did slip ashore to explore the street stalls piled with limes and bananas, oranges and unknown fruits and vegetables, play tag and soldiers with the local black loons and peer curiously into the fly-swarming huts, until one day his foot was bitten by something he never even saw. The painful swelling, which of course he had to hide from Maxwell, convinced him that Iain was right. He was safer on the ship. But that didn't mean he had to miss his chances.

He raided the captain's belongings. Two bottles of wine, a fruit cake—with rat droppings artistically left in the tatters of the oiled paper wrappings—four jars of plum jam; a pair of scissors, stockings, a tie-pin, and several other small items that could have been lost, broken or worn out. In exchange he got a dozen small pearls and a little nugget of gold, which he stitched inside the waistband of his new sailcloth breeches. In America, they would give him a start as a trader.

Black porters in single file like ants carried off the trade goods on their heads from the hold to Mister Lopez's warehouses. Then the sleeping shelves were rebuilt, stronger than before. Heavy iron rings were bolted into them, 'For to chain the blackies down,' the carpenter explained.

Meanwhile the stores were refilled with sacks of corn-meal and foreign vegetables, yams and plantains, to feed the slaves on the voyage. River water was pumped into the empty water casks; when Dand commented on its muddiness, he was told, 'It'll do fer niggers!'

Dand and Iain once went to the outskirts of the town to see a barracoon. 'Man, it's twice the size o' the Aberdeen cattle mart!' Dand commented, awed by the long rows of men and women chained between posts. 'Three times. An' there's more like this? Man!'

Other ships arrived, but the *Daisy* had a six-day start on them. 'We'll stow the morn,' Maxwell beamed, 'an' be off first tide next day. Six hundred prime blacks, an' we're first away! Man, what a price we'll get in Jamaica!'

Six hundred? Dand gaped. How would they get them all in?

He soon found out. An endless line of naked men tramped down the wharf at dawn, their neck rings tied to a long rope. The sailors riveted them in pairs, ankle to ankle in a solid iron fetter, and then drove them hobbling up the gangplank and down the ladder to the hold. Beaten on by the crew's cudgels and tripped by the fetters, some fell, dragging their partners crashing with them. One broke a leg and was sent back.

Below, Dand helped pack them. They had to slide awkwardly in on their sides, their feet against the outer hull, all facing forward, close against each other like spoons with no room to roll over, twice as tight as the Highlanders. Their shoulders almost filled the gap between the shelves. The sailors used spiked sticks to force them in, clanking and wailing, until each shelf was jammed full. Then a chain was run through a loop in the neck rings and padlocked to the rings in the shelves, and that was them safe.

All that could be seen of the slaves was a row of sweat-shiny faces and woolly hair, desperate eyes rolling, red mouths yelling or crying, and hands waving in helpless plea or anger. They looked daft, Dand thought, but he couldn't laugh the way most of the crew did.

When no more could be forced into the shelves, the lower hatches were lifted so that others could be jammed in on top of the food stored below the lower deck. 'They'll have more room later, as the food's eaten. It aye takes an age at first, till they learn their places,' Robb complained. Then the rest were packed along the centre. These could sit, and stand up or climb over each other to get nearer the grating over the hatchway to breathe. The heat and airless stink were already suffocating in the hold; what must it be like for the men wailing underneath it, beating on the lower hatches whose gratings were now covered with bodies?

By late afternoon the men were packed in, and the women and children arrived. They were pushed into the forward part of the hold, right up in the bows, which had been partitioned off. As they hurried past trying to dodge the prying, poking hands, the crew picked the ones they fancied. 'This fat quine's a good handful, eh, Dand?' Iain cried cheerfully.

Dand wasn't listening. Lopez's carriage was standing on the wharf. The captain was talking to Lopez, nodding, looking across at Dand, who somehow was not surprised when the captain jerked his head to call him. 'There he is, then,' Maxwell announced to Lopez. 'Clean an' healthy, like I told ye.'

Dand froze, his scalp crawling as Lopez's black eyes studied him like a snake with a frog. 'That red hair. Unusual. Intriguing. Thank you, sir captain.' He smiled to Dand. 'Come, boy.'

'C-come?' Dand stammered. 'Sir—sir, what d'ye mean?'

'Here's yer new master, loon. He won ye from me at cards last night.' Grinning, Maxwell clipped Dand's ear. 'Ye'll no' steal from him the way ye have from me, ye wee hellion! Did ye think I'd no' notice, ye impudent, thievin' whelp? I'm no' blind, nor daft.'

'No—no, sir! Please, no! Beat me, but don't leave me here! I'll run away—'

'Accept it, boy,' Lopez advised, not unkindly. 'You will be well treated. Run? A white in a town of blacks, my own town, you cannot hide. Do not—ah, foolish!'

Dand had fled up the gangplank, but Mister Robb caught him. Roughly, a sailor tied his hands behind him. Lopez watched him kicking, and sighed. 'Bring him after me.'

'Aye, sir.' Robb shrugged when he met Dand's eye. 'Davie, Iain. Take him along.'

Maxwell glared at them. 'Lose him an' I'll see yer backbones!'

Dand was dragged off behind the slowly-moving carriage, struggling vainly, pleading, 'No! Please, sir! Help me, Iain! Davie, loose me! Ye'll no' do this—no' to a friend, a white man!'

'Let ye go? Ye think Maxwell didn't mean it? Ye're mad!' Davie laughed. 'Shut yer gab, ye wee tink!'

'Sorry, Dandy. Ah'd help if Ah could, but . . . ' Iain muttered, head down.

At last they turned in through a high gate, up a path to a big house with deep verandahs. Lopez spoke in Portuguese to two blacks, who took charge of Dand. 'Traitors!' he howled at his former friends. Davie laughed; Iain slunk away, ashamed.

Dand was hauled along a path behind the house, past several huts with black people staring from the doors, and thrust still tied inside a small hut some distance from the rest. As the door shut and the bar dropped outside, he hurled himself at it, kicking at it. Outside a deep voice commented, to laughter and then silence.

Nobody came to his shouts. Nobody came . . . Nobody came . . .

At least in Aberdeen his captors had been his own colour, spoke his own language. Here he was alone, in the power of strangers. How would they act? Did the blacks eat white boys?

He'd not give in. He'd escape! He must!

How?

Suddenly the bar scraped. Dand tensed.

It was not Lopez. An old man came in, talking a soothing gabble, set down a bowl with some porridge, and gestured to Dand to turn round to let his wrists be freed.

Though Dand's hands were stiff and swollen, he almost tried to grab the bowl and brain the old man, but thought better of it at the sound of voices outside. Trying to smile, rubbing life back into his fingers, he pointed to the door, mimed lifting the bar, pointed to himself, acted slipping out and running away. The man chuckled, shaking his head— but when Dand began to rip with his teeth at his canvas belt, he looked interested.

Dand squeezed out three pearls, and held them out, repeating the mime. The old man shook his head, but more slowly. Dand winkled out another. The man looked doubtful. At last, as a sixth pearl emerged, he nodded. Then he snatched the pearls from Dand's hand, and scuttled out. The bar slammed down.

'Damn ye, ye thieving rogue! May ye sit on the hot hob o' hell for a thousand year!' What now? Damn them all! Dod, he could cry like a bairn!

No! He'd fight! Gritting his teeth, Dand picked up the bowl and scooped the porridge into his mouth with his fingers. He must eat, for strength.

He had not expected to sleep, but when, much later, the bar was stealthily lifted again, he woke with a jump. The door scraped quietly over the earth floor. Dand tensed, ready to attack. No one came in. A hand, dimly lit by moonlight, beckoned. Dand gulped—but what had he to lose?

The old man was there, fingers to his lips. Silently he replaced the bar and led Dand creeping back to the road. He pointed to the left, murmuring in his own tongue. Dand hesitated, but the old man had kept the silent bargain and let him out; why should he urge him in the wrong direction? 'Thank ye!' Dand whispered. 'God bless ye! I'm sorry I miscalled ye! I thank ye kindly!' He shook the old man's hand. The man looked astonished, grinned, nodded and scurried off.

It was that quick, that simple. The man must have felt a kindness for him, to risk at least a whipping if he was discovered. But what now?

Hide his whiteness. A handful of mud did that, smeared over Dand's face and arms. He had learned young, stealing apples from the Big House at home, that if you slunk along guiltily folk noticed you more, so although he kept to the moonlight shadows he went steady. His heart was thumping to shake him.

Terrified of hungry ghosts and gods, the blacks stayed sheltered withindoors at night, so to Dand's relief there were few people about, though voices arguing, shouting, laughing, babies crying and watchdogs barking from the huts and houses he passed made him jump and tremble.

He'd not been brought this far—had he? He was lost . . .

The dank smell of rot strengthened. And that moaning— that was the slaves in the hold. He knew that twisted palm tree—round here—aye, there was the water, and the ship.

Where was he going, anyway? Maxwell would just send him back, and he couldn't stay here—the Lopez man was right, he'd stand out like dandruff on a black coat. There were seven other ships in. Three were Portuguese, one

French, two Dutch, one American where at least they would speak English. But he would have to hide till they left; they might well hand him back to Lopez as an escaping slave. And they had only just arrived, they might be here for weeks yet. Anyway, they were anchored out in the river, away from the wharf. Did he dare swim to them, among the sharks?

No.

The *Daisy* was leaving at dawn. If he could stay hidden for a week, Maxwell wouldn't turn back with him. He'd beat him, of course, but it would still be better than staying with the Lopez man.

Dand crouched behind an upturned canoe, almost tripping over a black man sleeping there, and studied the ship. The slaves' moaning would cover any noise he made. No light in the captain's cabin; was he asleep or ashore? Ashore, making the most of his last night on land like most of the crew, for the watchman was awake, leaning on the bulwarks near the bowsprit, beside the lantern. He would see nothing when he turned away from it. Aye, Dand could slip aboard, if only something would draw the man's attention.

Dand eyed the black man snoring at his feet. Sorry—but it had to be done!

He kicked him awake and started to shout at him. 'Ye damned thief! Get out o' here or I'll have ye whipped!' He cursed and swore in his deepest voice, kicking the man to his feet, threatening him with a stick. Fuddled with sleep, the man scrambled up and fled along the river bank, tripping noisily over a dog that leapt up barking, making as much distraction as a herd of cows.

While the sentry peered after the running man, Dand slipped down to the end of the jetty, leapt the two-metre gap to the bulwarks of the poop and slithered over. Before the dockside fuss died away he took off his shirt and rolled it into a loose bundle round his hand. Holding it on his shoulder, hiding his face, he trotted down the ladder to the main deck and into the cabin passageway, like a sailor on an errand. Done it! Now to hide away safe, and he knew just where!

He opened the captain's cabin door and stopped dead.

'In the name o' the Wee Man! Dand!' By Maxwell's bed Iain was sitting up, mouth agape.

'Let me hide! Don't give me away!' Dand whispered urgently. 'Please, Iain!'

Iain hesitated. 'Dod, Maxwell'll slay ye!'

'Better that than Lopez.'

'Aye, fine for you, but he'd murder me as weel!' Scared, Iain was poised to shout. 'Ah'll no' risk that for ye!'

'Here. Here.' Dand fumbled with his belt, to get out the gold nugget. 'Here. You take it. Please, Iain!'

At last, after another age of hesitation, Iain nodded. 'Aye, right, loon.' He stowed the nugget away in his waistband. 'Ah'm the brute's new cabin-boy. Where will ye hide—so Ah dinna find ye, eh?'

Gratefully, Dand winked. 'I'll tuck in back o' the big box under Maxwell's bed. Ye never seen me slip in—an' ye can find me in a week or so, that'll maybe put him off beltin' ye.'

'Under his very bed! Dod, ye're crazy!' But Iain started to laugh. 'Man, will he no' be wild! I must see this, eh? His face—it'll be worth a beltin'! Come on, he could be back any time.' He helped haul the sea-chest out to let Dand slide behind it, and shoved it back in with a grunt and a giggle. 'Ah'll bring ye water. Luck, loon!'

LINK THIRTEEN
Juliet and Dand:
April–May

———

Forty paddlers brought the king's representative on the third day, rowed along the coast in a canoe bigger than Juliet had imagined possible. The official himself sat on a raised throne, under a vast red umbrella with a fringe of swinging, glittering glass beads.

Though the crew paraded to honour him they were well armed, and the ship's guns were ready loaded and tilted to point as far down as possible against attacking canoes. Beyond cocking a knowing eye at the guns the visitors ignored the precautions.

The official was tall and muscular, the finest man Juliet had ever seen, in a short dragon-embroidered Japanese coat of yellow silk and a cocked hat bristling with a huge fan of peacock feathers. As he climbed the boarding ladder he radiated an impressive calm authority, despite his bare legs. Behind him came several spearmen wearing nothing but beads and a skirt of monkey tails.

Juliet was glad to find that she was not blushing.

'Sixty pounds each on the block in Charleston!' Hunt hissed. 'More for the big buck!'

She frowned. Turn this heroic figure into a plantation hand? Demeaning. Offensive.

The boats had been launched, leaving space for a long cabin to be built right along the main deck. The spars, lowered and lashed between the masts, supported a thatch of palm leaves over strong slatted walls built along the deck, with a narrow passage on each side. 'Luxury, eh? But it lets the demned niggers settle, stops 'em panickin' or gettin' too seasick later,' Hunt had explained.

The officer settled on a chair in the airy shade, casually flirting a white zebra-tail fly-whisk with a carved ivory handle. Bob Bigtooth translated for him. 'King man say you give dash now, sir.'

Owens signed to Juliet. She offered a musket, powder and shot, a full anker of gerebita, a brass coal-scuttle full of glass beads, shirts, and lengths of checked cloth until the official nodded satisfaction. The guards got dash, too—a knife each, a bell, a clay pipe, and a twist of tobacco.

Gifts for the king were produced; a much-gilded china dinner service, a silver-plated helmet with red and white ostrich plumes—Bert, who had spent days polishing it, mourned to lose its glory—and a pump organ. 'Rot to bits in three months, an' out of tune, sounds like a demned pig-sticking, but the savages can't play it in any case,' Hunt sneered.

Pint mugs of gerebita were tossed back like thimbles of water while the king's tax was negotiated. 'Hundred pound, sir,' Bob declared, 'hundred musket, an' powder an' shot for go wid 'em.'

'That's more than ever before!' Captain Owens protested. Three hours and two gallons later they agreed on thirty, plus thirty red army coats and three barrels of rum.

Meanwhile, the spearmen wandered round, puffing their pipes, eyeing the swivel guns. Two of these small hand-cannon loaded with grape-shot had been fitted on stands on the poop facing down towards the main deck, in case of riot. A sailor stood by each to prevent accidents—or treachery.

When the king's man was at last fed and drunken and ready to leave, he called his guards. One of them casually tapped out his pipe beside the touch-hole of a swivel.

Two handfuls of gravel-sized lead shot blasted a head-sized hole through the wooden wall and deep into the deck planking, showering the king's man with splinters.

Spears and blunderbusses swung up—but the captain and the official were already shouting to their men, and managed to restore peace before battle started.

Owens dug the splinters out of the official's legs and

bandaged him up. To Juliet's amazement the man never once winced.

'Told you, sir! Don't feel pain!' Hunt whispered.

Graciously accepting a whole anker of gerebita to apologize for the bad manners of the gun, the king's officer waved his fly-whisk. The head guard speared the idiot whose folly had embarrassed and could have killed his lord. Everyone grinned as the scavenging sharks, waiting for rubbish thrown overboard, fought over this unexpected meal. Justice had been done. All was friendly again.

Juliet had never seen a dead person before, except when she was taken in to kiss her grandfather in his coffin, all clean, clove-scented, cold, not casually violent and gaudy and stinking of sweat and blood and guts. Her stomach heaved, her head spun . . .

Hunt's hand slid under her arm, supporting her. 'Brace up, Mister Smethwick, sir! Mustn't let 'em think we're demned soft!' He was hiding a sneer with a smirk.

She clenched her teeth. She'd not be sick! Not now. And never in front of him!

Trading began next day, on the shore. To avoid disease or accident Captain Owens forbade the crew to go inland past the small village of black traders which sprang up to serve them. Juliet didn't mind; it was too hot and sticky to go venturing far into the fields or the damp forest beyond, and the huge insects were abominable! She was interested in people, not plants, like Tony, and had no desire to go exploring for the legendary Great River, a branch of the Nile, which was said to run west to east—or maybe east to west, no one knew—far to the north. The round native huts, with their wicker walls and happy, roly-poly babies, were as far as she wanted to go. The birds were brilliant, but their cries were harsh, not musical; some could learn to talk, and a few of the sailors bought them, and monkeys, but she did not. She did buy a carved wood idol, and blushed when Jim told her, chuckling, 'Dat for make woman have boy baby!'

Jim sent coffles shuffling down to the ship, twenty or so

slaves a day at first. Juliet learned rapidly not to look in their eyes. She could withstand the pitiful pleading, the despair, the pain—but only if she didn't look in their eyes. They were merchandise, she told herself firmly. Not people. They'd be better off among Christians than in the jungle. They were absolutely necessary. They'd soon settle down and be content.

Just don't look in their eyes . . .

Six weeks later, she stood under a palm tree beside Mister Hunt and gazed round under the broad brim of her straw hat.

To one side, four slaves were being freed from a rope, the first coffle in a week. By now, Jim was bringing in small traders from inland, with maybe only two or three prisoners each. One by one, the blacks were dragged forward, usually terrified of the white faces. Juliet's job, with Hunt or Cartwright, was to examine them carefully for any defects to report to the captain, who lounged in a hammock under the palms, bargaining through Jim and Bob with the trader for each one.

Nearby a brazier burned, heating irons to brand the bought slaves. Some screamed; others suffered in proud or sullen silence. An iron ring was riveted round their necks, while likely troublemakers were manacled and fettered in pairs.

'Jim's done us proud!' Hunt commented. 'Sail about for months, rot me if you can't, huntin' a demned cargo, but we've got two hundred an' eighty already, an' two-thirds men. Why we're here, o' course. In a fort or a town you pay a demned fortune in dash, an' the king makes you buy all his slaves before you can trade with anyone else. Rubbish, most of 'em, an' demned dear, too!' He gestured to the young man they had just been examining, slumped at their feet. 'But look at this fellow! We'll get him for—oh, say ten pounds, an' sell him for forty. An' we've wax, ain't we?'

Juliet nodded. 'Almost a ton already. And ninety-four elephant teeth.'

'Should be a demned good trip. Whoo, rot this heat!' Puffing, Hunt fanned himself and scratched round under his breeches at the itching lice and heat rash.

'A ship costs perhaps £10,000 to fit out.' Juliet shook her head in wonder.

Hunt grinned. 'A mountain o' money, sir! But with a smart captain she can pay for herself in two or three trips, an' then she's a demned goldmine. If she's lucky!'

Trying to distract herself from the wailing and screams, from the latrine stink, the scorched skin, and the strangely heavy smell of black sweat, from the fear and shame of the youth at her feet, Juliet asked, 'Is the song true, then? "Beware, beware, the Bight of Benin, for one comes out for five that went in"?'

'Five? More like ten. It's hell here. Hell.' He waved his palmetto fan to summon a girl with a calabash of beer. 'Fire, blacks attackin', mutiny, shipwreck, pirates, storm, groundin', riot, a dozen diseases, rottin' to bits waitin' for a cargo or just demned bad luck—any demned thing can happen.'

Hunt lifted the calabash. 'That's why we buy these. Filthy demned country, eh? Fruit like wood! But tough enough for feedin' bowls an' spoons, an' safer. I've seen a man's brains dashed out with a wooden plate.' He grunted. 'Can't trust niggers, rot 'em! Try every demned way to escape.'

'Wouldn't you, sir?' Juliet asked wryly. 'If you were captured and enslaved?'

He merely huffed at her. 'That's different! I ain't black! You mind what I say, Smethwick! Demned sly, they are, God rot 'em, aye, an' the women help 'em. Any piece o' metal can be sharpened to a knife, even a demned spoon. Any bit o' wood can be a bludgeon. One mistake, an' you're dead! Never let your pistol out o' hand's reach. It can save you.' He patted the long pistols in his own belt. 'An' keep your eyes open. With experience, you can spot demned bad 'uns early. See that big buck they're runnin' along the beach? He'll give trouble—I knew it! Bird up!'

The man whose agility was being tested had broken free. With a wrestler's twist he broke the neck of one of Jim's guards, and was racing away. Not even rising, Hunt drew one of his pistols, aimed, and fired. The man stumbled and fell, coughing blood, his face ploughing along the sand.

'On the wing! Demned good shot, eh?' At Hunt's feet, the youngster whimpered in fear. 'Teach the rest to behave!'

'Mister Hunt! Do not waste the goods!' Owens called.

'We hadn't paid for him, sir!' Hunt called back.

'Ah. That's all right, then. God save his soul. Bring that one up.'

Swallowing hard, Juliet stood up as Hunt kicked the young black to his feet and prodded him towards the captain. 'You can manage without me, sir. There's a canoe ready to take the first ones aboard. I'll go with them and send in some more cloth.' She had to get away . . .

A woman with a baby was struggling by the canoe. 'Come on, sir!' the bosun called. He held the woman while Juliet splashed knee-deep and climbed in. Then he snatched the baby and tossed it to Juliet. Defeated, the woman scrambled after her child, to collapse among the blacks already in the boat. 'Which niggers 'andles easy if ye knows the tricks! You 'ang on to that brat, sir, acos if she gets 'old of it she could throw 'erself over, tryin' to escape, but she won't while you got it. Don't want 'er to drown 'erself, do we?'

'Not when she's paid for,' Juliet agreed bitterly, trying not to drop the wriggling, screaming child as the black paddlers heaved the canoe leaping out through the surf. It was always a thrill, even now.

The sailors laughed, accepting her words as a joke. 'Right, sir, right! Ye're learnin'!' The bosun tapped his nose confidentially. 'Which some on us thought at first as ye mightn't 'ave the guts for the trade. Some on us—' he sneered at one of his mates, '—said as ye was one o' them snivellin' god-damned nosy-parkerin' anti-slavers. But I says as ye're the right stuff—quiet an' genteel, never toppin' the nob, a proper gennelman, but tough inside, a real man! If I may make so bold, sir.'

'Er—thank you.' How wrong could he be? Tough; that was a joke. Squeamish and sentimental, mawkish, just like a girl, all the things she despised . . .

But did she want to be like Hunt? Or even the captain?

On board, she headed for the poop, where the trade goods had been stacked to let the carpenters build slave decks in the hold. In the central shack a quarter of the slaves already bought were sitting about in their turn on deck, mostly miserable but apathetic, finishing off their bowls of boiled yams. One man had been whipped for refusing to eat, but the rest had learned from that; the mouth openers had not been needed. A sailor was playing the flute to them—it helped calm them down—and Bob the linguist was making some work the pump, hosing down the decks and each other with sea water. As Captain Owens said, the devil makes work for idle hands, the sooner they learned to obey and be useful the better, and this made them see that care was being taken of them. The worst score or so who refused to surrender, struggling, shouting and clashing their chains, were kept below separate from the rest. They'd not be let on deck till they quietened.

Juliet walked along beside the hut wall. A barricade was built across the ship by the mainmast, across both the hold and the deck cabin, to separate men, kept forward of it, from the women aft. Some were talking to each other through it. Wives and husbands? Did blacks have their own kind of marriage? Hunt said not, no more than cows, but Captain Owens said they bought their wives, so the women were only exchanging one kind of slavery for another. It didn't matter, anyway; it was not a Christian union, and they would probably be split up when they were sold. Poor souls . . .

Stop that!

Were they planning a revolt? If they were, they'd fail. Muskets and blunderbusses were loaded and racked ready for use, and the swivels were ready, too.

Rummaging among her crates, she glanced up at a cry. 'Ship runnin' in, sir, from the east!'

A score of ships had paused briefly to gossip. Even to Juliet's inexpert eye this one looked dirty, and the slave stink and moan from her was enough to turn your stomach. However, despite her slovenly appearance the new arrival spilled the wind neatly from her sails and hung drifting about fifty metres away.

Mister Cartwright, officer of the watch, squeezed between two stacks of crates to shout greetings through his speaking-trumpet. 'Ahoy, *Daisy*! Any news?'

'How's the markets?' the captain of the *Daisy* called, in a Scottish accent. They exchanged gossip. Plenty stock now in Angola—the *Daisy* hoped to catch the markets with the first of them. Yellow fever in Bonny, smallpox in Fort James. A girl in Jamaica had fetched almost three hundred pounds! French privateers were out in the West Indies.

As Juliet listened, someone touched her sleeve. 'Shir! 'Ere, shir!' Finger to his lips, Bert beckoned her over to the far side of the poop and jerked his head over the bulwarks. She glanced over, and stiffened. Below her, clinging desperately to the stern anchor rope, was a boy. A black boy—no, a white one, but black with bruises head to toe, with blood oozing from weals and broken skin. A triangular fin was gliding in . . .

He must be running from the *Daisy*. Bert was tying a loop in the end of a coil of rope. 'Quick, shir, or shark'll get 'im. An' quiet, eh?'

She must save the boy, of course, but should she not tell Cartwright? Bert wanted her to keep quiet. What was the right thing to do?

Get the boy up first. No one was watching. She nodded. Bert tossed the rope down to the boy, who slung it over his head and arms and launched himself for the ship's side, the fin shooting after him, the ripping gape opening sideways . . . But she and Bert hauled and the boy clawed fingers and toes at every ridge and crack, scrabbling frantically up, away

121

from the teeth, till he slithered over the bulwarks. Frustrated, the shark swirled away.

Had the officers seen? No; they were masked by a stack of cowrie hampers.

The boy gasping at her feet looked up with bright blue eyes. She barely recognized the thick, guttural accent as English. 'Let me stay, sir, for dod's sake! Or he'll murder me!' She winced as she studied him; she could well believe it.

Behind her there was a sudden shout. 'Dand! Where's that loon? Hey, *Kestrel*, has a loon—a white lad—come aboard ye? He's run, damn him! I'll flay his hide! Ye'll send him back, ye hear me! I paid good silver for him! I'll slay him! Who's that lad I can see there? Is that him? Are ye stealin' him?'

'Who is it, Smethwick?' Cartwright called, rather stiff at the accusation.

By Juliet's knee a hole gaped and shut. The boy had gone. Bert sat on the block of wood where he had hidden from the press, wiped a foot over a red puddle on the deck and winked.

Return a boy to be murdered? No! Suddenly sure of herself, she turned. 'I can only see Bert, sir, but there's a shark all excited by the anchor chain, and blood in the water!' Not a word of a lie . . .

===============

Captain Maxwell sailed on west, angrily accepting that his young slave was dead. However, that evening Captain Owens was furious.

From a cot in the sick bay, for he was too weak to stand, Dand explained. 'Ah'd have stayed wi' Captain Maxwell, sir. As the Lord's ma witness, Ah would so. But he went fair mad, sir, when he found me. Clean crazy. Near beat me tae death, an' the same again every day. He swore he'd slay me for breakin' his word. But Ah never gave my word, sir!' Ashamed of his weakness, he wiped away tears and snot with the back of his hand. 'He'd do it. Or bring me back next trip, he said, for to hand me back, sir, an' pay his gamblin' debts.'

Owens considered, his face cold. At length he nodded. 'Since we have you, I shall tend your wounds—until I can return you to your master.'

'No, sir! Ah beg ye!' Dand gasped.

Owens was unmoved. 'The law requires me not to assist any slave to escape. It makes no mention of colour or nationality.' Pausing to see that the boy would not dare argue any further, the captain nodded. 'However, it does not demand that I go out of my way to return him. The *Daisy* was bound for Jamaica? We are heading for Charleston. If through the Lord's will we do not encounter your master again, and if you should evade my ship in port, I am under no obligation to chase you.' He ignored the dawning hope and joy on Dand's face, and stalked out.

'Thank ye, sir! God bless you!' Dand lay back, wincing, almost sobbing with restored hope. There was kindness in there, under the captain's stern face.

In the main cabin, Juliet and Bert saw none of it.

'You, boy. A dozen strokes with a cane where they'll do

123

most good. Then you will spend your daytime at the fore crosstrees for a month unless you are called on for duty. No rum until then, either. You may go.' As he scuttled out, Bert's face showed his dismay; the beating was a passing nuisance, perching on a cross-spar for hours was painful, boring, and tiring, but the rum was a sore loss.

Juliet braced herself. Her turn now.

'How dare you, Mister Smethwick?' Owen's voice was cutting.

'The boy was kidnapped, sir!' she protested.

'So he claims. Have you heard the other side of the case? For all we know he is a legally bound apprentice, due imprisonment for breaking his contract—and the same for anyone who aids him! Or a transported convict, escaping or allowed out under licence!'

'But his injuries, sir—in Christian charity—'

'You dare instruct me, sir? He might well be a thief or brawler. Is he likely to admit to either? Did you think of that? Did you think at all? You aided a slave, the property of another man, to abscond.'

'He's white, sir!'

'Be silent, sir! You lied by misdirection, aided one of my crew to deceive his superior officer, smuggled a possibly dangerous ruffian aboard my ship, made me confederate in your dishonesty! Your lack of moral fibre disappoints me, sir. Your father will be no more impressed than I.'

Knowing that everyone within earshot of the cabin windows and door was avidly eavesdropping, Juliet gritted her teeth to stop herself snapping at him. Owens eyed her coldly. 'Until further notice, your every leisure moment you will spend in your cabin, and contemplate your sins!'

'Yes, sir.' Juliet turned away stiffly. She was glad to go. In the tiny cubby-hole she would at least have privacy to curse—or cry. What would Grandmama Smethwick think of this?

* * *

124

About twenty miles inland, on that same day, Gbodi hid her joy when the leader of the slavers fell ill. All was happening as Omu had said—oh, wise Omu! Her helpfulness and smiles made everyone trust her. When she cautiously added filth to the stewpots, no one suspected that she was causing the illness. Her gods were with her.

Hassan was terrified. He was months away from home, wandering through a sticky, stinking, mosquito- and leech-ridden swamp, the slaves weak and sick, and his father usually either raving or unconscious. Everything rested on his shoulders.

Uzum had carried a springy cane, more a sign of authority than a weapon. Hassan used it, though, working off his fear and frustration on slaves, paddlers, and guards alike, lashing out till the guards were mutinous and the guides in revenge led him astray into the mangrove swamps where there was no solid ground to camp and cook on, and then ran off. He was constantly afraid; his father's knife was always in his sash, his musket by his hand. But what else could he do? He mustn't fail! He had to hide his panic. He must reach the sea! Nothing must stop him!

Day after weary day he drove them on, ill with tension, struggling south through the tangled swamp. The water began to rise and fall, and tasted of salt. Uzum, in a conscious spell, told him it was the tide. 'We are near the sea, father? Praise to Allah!'

'O Help of the helpless, help me, guide me . . . ' As he raised his head from prayers one morning a canoe appeared from the dark mangroves. It turned in towards the moored canoes where Uzum lay shivering on his mat. The guards tensed, but the strangers were smiling, showing open hands. A man gestured towards the forty-three slaves tied in the canoes, and in fairly correct Hausa said straight out, '*Salaam*. My name is Tafawa Jimoh. I buy slaves.'

In spite of the man's rude abruptness, Hassan almost fell on his neck with relief.

125

Awake for once, Uzum agreed faintly. 'Certainly all occurs as Allah wills.'

'Slave are sick, many die soon. Twenty cabess for one slave, if I buy all, ' Jimoh offered.

What a relief, to be rid of them all! No; think! Hassan pulled himself together, tried to keep his wits about him. 'No, it is too little! *Ya Allah*, they are only tired with travel, and will soon recover.' He nodded at a little girl who had been very helpful during the last few days. 'This girl is a good worker, friendly and willing and always healthy. I'd want thirty iron manillas for her alone.'

Jimoh shook his head. 'Could king pay so much? Not me! But you know sea, ship, white man? Certainly white man buy slave, and elephant tooth. White man are foolish, pay high price. You dash me fifty manilla, I guide you. White man have fine trade goods, many musket, powder. Agreed?'

He'd see white men after all! 'Ten manillas.' They settled on twenty. Grinning, Hassan brandished his cane. 'Gunpowder, father! A great profit, and we'll see the sea and white men! *Ya Allah!* Praise to the One who guides all those who trust in Him, and Muhammad his Prophet, blessings be upon Him! Move, everyone!'

The paddlers, happy that at last someone knew where they were going, dug in to follow the stranger. Away in the back of Hassan's mind a faint worry was gibbering that this was a bad idea, something was wrong. But he was too relieved to listen to it.

For three hours they followed the stranger, as the winding channel widened, the trees above fell away. Everyone clutched the canoe sides as long, slow waves began to roll past them. The paddlers occasionally fell into clattering confusion until they learned how to deal with the swell. Then the shores slowly curved away to each side, opened out to a vast, terrifying nothing ahead but blue, not brown, water.

Some of the slaves screamed. So did some of the guards.

'Careful! Not turn over in wave!' Cheerfully Jimoh

beckoned Hassan to the right, inside the surf but outside the mangrove trees which grew right out into the sea. After another hour, the mangroves drew back from the water's edge, and a sandy beach appeared. 'We walk now. Not far.'

Jimoh gave them no time to chatter; he led them off along the water's edge, a straggling line carrying the elephants' teeth and Uzum on his mat. At least it was firm sand underfoot, not foul, squelchy mud. Then, as they crossed a headland, Hassan stopped dead. In front of them a house was floating. No, a ship. What a wonder!

Men were standing on the shore. Red-skinned, not white like his grandmother; but their loose hair was streaky brown, their eyes pale as ghosts'. Some of the guards hissed in fright, but Jimoh called to reassure them. 'Certainly no fear! This are the white man!'

He went forward to meet the approaching red men, grinning and joking in his broken English. 'Jim good man, eh? Say me get plenty slabe!' As he talked, the red— white—men began to grin too.

Hassan found, to his pleasure, that he could understand a word or two. His grandmother had told him true! Soon he would tell the white men about her, and they would talk and eat together, and maybe he could go out and see over the big ship.

A canoe sped out through the surf towards the floating house. 'He go get musket, powder for you,' Jimoh explained in his bad Hausa, grinning encouragingly. 'Now you come, I talk for you to white man, you sell slave for many goods.'

Crouched as usual by Uzum's side, Gbodi was watching carefully. Some of the other slaves were terrified of the red ghosts, but that was stupid. She would not be fattened and eaten, Omu had told her so. She trusted his words absolutely. Her gods were still with her. Maybe they had sent these pale-eyed people to help her get revenge on the bully who had beaten Omu and separated them.

A young man walked past. Start now . . . She beamed up at him.

127

For a week Juliet had scarcely seen daylight. She hadn't spoken to Bert at all. The sailors liked Dand, but mostly condemned her action. Mister Cartwright was furious because she had tricked him. Hunt offered smarmy applause for her boldness and compassion. As Owens had advised, she spent the time thinking, and her thoughts were not pleasant. To meet such a friendly, beaming smile lifted her spirits. This child—yes, she was a branded slave, but she seemed happy; maybe being a slave wasn't always as horrible as Juliet had almost decided. She smiled back.

Hassan was delighted with the prices he negotiated for the slaves and the ivory. The slaves were quickly examined, rebranded, some for the third or fourth time, and chained. They screamed at the touch of iron instead of rope; it seemed the final sign that they would never go home.

When Gbodi was called she went docilely, but stiffened at the weight of the neck ring. She had somehow believed that she was safe, that she would escape and get home; it had almost been like a new bubble round her, burst by this cold clasp of iron. But she calmed herself; Omu had not said that she would be safe, not exactly. He had told her to try to escape, and to fight. That was her true protection; that she would act, not weep. If she had to bear the iron, she would, and not scream and wail.

Almost absently, she knelt beside the anvil. The hammer clanged, riveting on her neck ring. Coldly, silently she rose, feeling the pressure, the burn at her neck, the pain of her latest branding; for this, they would pay.

The slaves around her eyed her uneasily. This child made them nervous. She was somehow not normal. She smiled, she had no fear. Was she mad?

The pale-eyed man at the brazier grinned and patted her shoulder, saying something approving. Gbodi beamed at him. Curse you . . .

She returned quietly to squat again beside Uzum and pick up her fan. Since she seemed calm, and was clearly not trying to run away, nobody stopped her.

When the last tusk was priced, the white lord beckoned a girl with a drink; Hassan stood up and walked down the beach to tell his father. Juliet smiled at him. He wasn't a slave; she could look in his eyes. '*Salaam*.' It meant 'Peace', Bob had told her.

Hassan bowed. '*Salaam aleikum*.' His father was asleep. This might be the person to start talking to, someone young like himself. He laid his precious musket down on the mat, off the sand, drew a deep breath, pointed to himself, and said carefully, 'I name Hassan. I dada—' he gestured to Uzum, '—I dada he mama name Bridie Treworthy, come out England. Out Turo, out Cornal.' He repeated it, slowly.

'Your dad—your father's mama came from where?' Juliet blinked. 'Turo? Cornal? Treworthy—that's a Cornish name. Truro, in Cornwall! Of course!' She felt elated.

Hassan nodded, beaming. Grandmother's words worked!

Almost giggling in surprise, taking Hassan's hand, Juliet turned him towards the captain who was coming down the beach towards them with Mister Cartwright. 'Sir, the boy here speaks a little English. His grandmother was from Truro, he says!'

'English? That will be useful, thank you, Mister Smethwick.' Owens's voice was abstracted.

The canoe had returned. A score of sailors jumped out, carrying belaying pins and muskets, running up the beach. 'Here's your dash,' Juliet began—and then stopped. The men were spreading out round Hassan's guards, one of whom, suspicious, raised his own musket. The bosun yelled, 'Get 'em, lads!' and the sailors dived forward, clubbing and wrestling the guards and paddlers to the sand.

'What—but—sir! This is treachery, sir!' Juliet screamed. 'No! How can you—?'

'You think you're at your mama's tea-party? Young fool!' Cartwright guffawed. 'Seventy-three slaves, for coppers! That fills us up. An' ivory! That's how to make a profit! Good man, Jim! We dash you plenty plenty!'

Behind him, Tafawa Jimoh was chortling, waving to his

own men to help the whites catch a few escapers. These people were only up-country strangers, nobody to offend and spoil the trade. It had been so simple, his acting skill scarcely needed to trick the young fool. He had led them like goats to slaughter. Now the white men would dash him enough to buy another wife, and along the shore, unknown to them, he had two good canoes to send trading up-river; so much profit, for no work, no outlay, no risk—excellent business!

On his mat, Uzum wakened in alarm. Seeing the fighting, he lifted Hassan's musket. A shot rang out—but he had not fired. Ach, his chest hurt . . . Uzum fell back, a look of utter surprise on his face. One dead hand flopped aside, striking Juliet's feet where she stood paralysed with shock.

Hassan found he was still holding the white youth's hand, and jerked away. Escape! Father—Allah, he is dead! Allah help me—run! Screaming in terror, he dodged Cartwright's grab, fled—

Crouching unnoticed, Gbodi stuck out a thin leg and tripped him. As he scrambled up she grabbed his sleeve and tugged his arm out from under him so that he fell again. Two sailors pounced on him and hauled him to his feet among shouts of, 'Got 'im! Get 'im down to the fire, lads! That's the last one!'

Hassan's staring, horrified eyes met Gbodi's over his father's body.

Sweetly, she smiled at him. She caught the eye of the young red-face, and smiled even more.

U nused to idleness, as soon as Dand was able to move with reasonable ease he got himself up and about. He made friends with the cook by helping to tend the cauldrons of brown horse-beans, big as his hand, with some lard and pepper, that were constantly cooking for the slaves as they came up eighty at a time. When the sailors began to dismantle the women's end of the hut, Dand was happily full of beans; with luck the *Daisy* would never be seen again.

Captain Owens was speaking to a gang of slaves newly dragged whimpering on board. 'We are not going to eat you,' Bob Bigtooth translated into three languages. 'We are taking you to dig the ground in our country, to grow crops for us. You will get food and water. You will be treated well if you behave well. If you behave badly, if you fight, or refuse to eat, or try to strike a white man, you will be punished. But do as you are told and you will not be hurt. Now here is food. Eat and rest.'

One boy started to scream hysterically, broken words of English. 'I no slave! I name Hassan! I dada he mama—' A sailor knocked him to the deck, sobbing. To Dand's surprise, some of the other new slaves attacked him as he lay, kicking and shouting at him until the sailors stopped them.

The slaves who had been on board for days started to line up by the hatch in the wall to get their calabashes of beans. They beckoned to the newcomers, many of whom had been half-starved for weeks and seemed astonished at the amount they got. When the food was finished, a flute struck up. 'Dance! Dance!' the sailors called. Sullenly, the men began to hop about; any who refused to exercise were hit with a knotted rope's end.

Dand helped drag the cauldron along to serve the women.

One woman was sitting by the outer wall, holding a sickly baby. When a sailor nudged her towards the food line she did not move. The man raised his rope, but a small girl slid in under it, flashing him a smile, and began to talk to the woman. 'Good lass!' the sailor said, and got such a beaming smile in return that he himself began to smile.

Always smiling, Gbodi whispered in the woman's ear. 'Smile, and obey them, and fight back when you can.' She must pass on what Omu had said. 'Our gods are still with us. Smile, learn what will help us fight the red ghosts. If you starve, you'll have no strength to fight. Eat now, grow strong!'

An older woman nearby translated, adding in her own tongue, 'The girl speaks sense. Smile and eat, and fight back when we have a chance of escaping.'

All the women gathering round murmured agreement. One of them began to sing with the flute: 'Smile and eat, grow strong! Eat, grow strong, smile!'

'Remember the black red man that knows our languages!' the older woman warned.

Still chanting, the singer nodded. 'Our gods are here. Eat, smile, grow strong!'

A woman hissed through the partition, 'Smile, eat, grow strong to fight them!'

Someone grunted in understanding. After a minute, the men's voices joined the song. The sailors relaxed, grinning. The men danced harder and harder, stamping their defiance, laughing, singing, shouting, 'Eat, grow strong, smile!'

Everyone began to look happier. Gbodi smiled. Omu was right; this was the way.

'Good niggers, this last lot. And that girl is demned helpful. No trouble this trip!' Hunt remarked.

The baby whimpered weakly. Gbodi put a small hand on the mother's arm. 'Blood for our freedom. It will die soon anyway. The gods will be pleased with the sacrifice, and help us.'

Quietly, calmly, the mother nodded, turned to where the

first panels of wicker wall had been torn down, and dropped the baby overboard, to vanish in a swirl of sharks.

One of the sailors shouted and pointed, but he was too late. The mother shrugged and silently joined the food line. The sailor spoke to the captain, who after a moment shrugged also. Dand could just hear him: 'It must have died. God rest its soul. Watch the woman. See she doesn't try to kill herself.'

Herself? Dand bit his lip. It wasn't herself his mother would kill if she was kidnapped and her bairn died. The captain knew blacks, must know what he was doing, but . . . Ladling out beans, he had noticed the women gathering round that queer-like wee quine. He'd keep an eye out for her. He didn't trust her. Her nor her bland smile.

A scuffle beside him made him jump. 'Oi, gerroff 'im!' A boy, dropping from the rigging, was driving three black men away from a youngster curled up in a corner of the deck. Dand jumped to help, and another couple of sailors shouted; the men backed away, leaving the lad sniffling.

'Don't like ye, eh?' Bert chuckled.

'You keep by us!' Dand encouraged the black loon. 'We'll keep ye safe!'

Wiping his nose on his forearm, Hassan tried to smile at the boys, fighting despair. He had half expected his father to die from the sickness, what was written was written, but not from being shot! He must find peace to say the funeral prayers . . . And being captured and chained, beaten like an animal . . . But certainly he must survive. He pointed to his chest. 'I Hassan! Hassan!'

'Hassan? That your name? Aye, well. Ah'm Dand.'

'I'm Bert.' Casually the boys patted Hassan's shoulder.

'Aye.' Dand looked more closely at Bert. 'Ye're the loonie as hauled me aboard, eh?'

'Loonie? Ye barmy gobbin! I'll knuckle yer 'ead for that!' Hassan jumped aside as they tussled. Were all white men crazy? But he still had to look to them for protection against his former guards. Allah pity him!

By the time the boys had sorted out the mistake they were good friends.

Nursing his bruises old and new, Dand cautiously followed Bert up to the cross-trees, beckoning Hassan to follow to a surprising haven of calm among the musical humming of the rigging, away from the anger, frustration, and despair on deck. Whenever he had time to spare he could be found there for the rest of Bert's sentence, and during Hassan's time on deck the black boy found that he was safe there from his former slaves. Dand understood half Bert's English; Bert understood less than half Dand's Scots; Hassan absorbed an oddly mixed language.

That same evening, though, Juliet was told to assist Mister Hunt in stowing the slave deck. She had only been there before during the day, when some of the slaves were on deck and the rest had room to sit and lie about, baking even though the hatches were left open. Now, with everyone below and the new slaves filling the space, it was more crowded than she had ever seen it. The sun was setting, huge and orange on the horizon. In the red light from above, the hold was like a hell swarming with demons.

'Short ones on the shelf an' up in the bows, tall ones down the middle, Mister Smethwick, sir. They'll be in here for two days while we re-rig the spars an' sails an' quit the demned coast. Fool niggers panic if they see the land goin' away, God rot 'em, try to throw 'emselves over an' swim back to shore. Seen 'em drown twenty at a time, mothers an' babies too, rot me if I ain't. Out at sea they're safe enough, don't know which demned way to swim! So now we pack 'em right an' tight, show 'em their places. You, up there!' Hunt gestured with his whip for a youth to jump onto the deep shelf where Dand was helping to pack them in.

'I no slave! I Hassan!' Hassan clutched at Juliet's arm.

'Hassan!' Dand recognized him casually. 'Come up, loon, smart now!'

While Juliet hesitated, Hunt knocked the boy's hand off her shirt sleeve and hit him. 'Ye'd dare touch a white man?

Get up, rot you—no, feet first!' Seeing no help for it, the boy jumped up and slithered onto the shelf. Hunt chuckled. 'Don't want to be a slave, I suppose! Demned idiot! Shove 'em up there, lad!'

'They're tight as beans in a barrel already!' Juliet protested.

Dand, bent double under the beams, kicked Hassan's feet closer to the next man and laughed. The blacks here had more headroom than the Highland emigrants, if no more lying space—and no freedom to move about, of course. 'Away, sir! Loose as a fisherwife's tongue! *Daisy*'s smaller nor this, but it's six hunder' niggers jammed bum to belly Captain Maxwell has, wi' two slave decks, no' the one.'

Bert was helping to pack the lower rows. 'We could do it, shir,' he said, 'but cap'n, 'e says no, we could lose 'alf on 'em.'

'Demned right too, God rot ye.' Hunt frowned at the possible criticism of the captain. 'Demned cholera can kill fifty a day when they're tight-packed.'

'Ain't argufyin', shir!' Bert protested. 'Shtink'd sicken a Shcotchman, too.'

'You mind yer tongue!' Dand popped his head over the edge to growl down, grinning at the teasing.

'Get on with it!' Hunt grunted, flourishing his whip.

Bert kicked the next man along, explaining, 'Shee, Mishter Shmethwick, shir, when they're packed that tight, iffen they goes to pish, them on each side slides in an' fills the shpace till they can't lie down again. Sho, they fouls an' pukes where they lies, shee, an' it shpills on them below. Same if they're chained down.'

Hunt agreed, battering the arms of a man who wanted to fight till the black slid moaning into his place. 'In bad weather, when you can't spare men from workin' the ship to guard 'em while you feed 'em, you keep 'em chained, not for two days, sir, like we'll do, but for weeks—get in, damn you! The muck sets round 'em like demned cement, 'pon me oath it does, till you can't see which are dead to get 'em out. Not till they start to bloat.'

135

' 'S right, shir,' Bert nodded. 'An' they rubs 'oles in their shoulders an' 'ips, from lyin' on 'em, an' it rots till ye can see the bones.' Juliet shuddered. Bert shook his head, pitying the young gent's weakness. 'Tough, some ships, shir! Got it easy 'ere!'

She looked round, coughing already in the hot smog, stinking of sweat and vomit and latrine barrels. Easy?

Jesus had said, 'Thou shalt love the Lord thy God . . . this is the first and great commandment. And the second is like, namely this, that thou shalt love thy neighbour as thyself.' Loving your neighbour was the same thing as loving God. If you did not do one, then you didn't do the other.

Uneasily she shrugged the thought away. These blacks were not her neighbours.

The women and children were allowed more room and more freedom, and by the captain's strict orders kept from any contact with the men, black or white. Once the ship was out of sight of land the children were allowed to roam fairly freely round the ship and the rigging, playing with Bert and Dand, cheering everyone up. Every day more of the men were unchained, until after three weeks all were freed. Everyone smiled, and ate, and grew strong.

In the women's cabin they discussed in whispers how Gbodi had been favoured and freed; how her masters had died; how she had caused the capture of the slaver youth; how she had told them to smile. Desperate for any hope, any hint of security, they decided that for sure she was a medicine woman. She was guarded by the other women, almost worshipped. They asked her what the gods wanted. What would Omu say? she thought, her eyes eerily blank, and told them, 'Help each other. Obey, smile, and be ready. Our chance will come.'

Luckily the trade winds stayed fair and the hatch covers could be kept constantly raised on banisters to allow air into the hold. A third of the men were allowed on deck at a time, for two hours twice a day, to get their food, take the air, and dance energetically to the flute and drums they made from

136

small kegs. Even the sailors standing constant guard at the swivels would clap and jig with them.

They were hosed down regularly with sea water, for Captain Owens insisted that it kept them healthier, in spite of the doubts of most of the crew. 'Three baths in yer life, sir,' Dand told Juliet sternly. 'When ye're born, when ye wed, an' when ye're buried. More's no good for ye. A good stinkin' sweat keeps off the plague, mam aye said.'

Juliet flattened him. 'I am supercargo. That means I'm in charge of the cargo. That means I'm responsible for its well-being. So I intend to see that it stays healthy—and despite what your mother said, that means clean!' The hold was hosed out and scrubbed with hot vinegar every week. She saw to that personally, and when the bosun protested at the work she withered him with a blast of cursing her grandmother would have been proud of. Genteel on the surface, eh? She'd show him!

Dand was surprised how little the *Kestrel* stank, compared to the *Daisy*. So was Juliet; it was little worse than the privy at home. She made sure it stayed that way.

For days Hassan desperately tried to come to terms with his fate. He was a slave! It was brutal, humiliating, wretched. Allah, why? Why? What had he done wrong, to be punished so?

When the captain called him, he was delighted. Now he would be recognized . . .

'You speak English?'

He did his best to show what he had learned. 'My dada his mama, she come from Truro, from Cornal—'

'Yes, yes. Is that all you know?' Owens waved him back, to Hassan's dismay. 'Mister Smethwick, on the voyage across to Charleston pray occupy yourself usefully by teaching some English to the brighter youngsters. Bob will assist you. This boy, and that smiling girl, and—Bob will suggest others.'

'Yes, sir.'

What would best help them? Juliet asked around, and

learned that she must teach not good English, but slave lingo. 'Or their masters'll think they're demned uppity, an' whip 'em,' Hunt informed her.

'Me good boy, massa, me sure 'nuff nebber goin' do nuffin' massa don' like!' Bob Bigtooth gave a demonstration. 'Dat's what de plantation overseers likes, Mister Smethwick, sir. You want to help 'em, you teach 'em to unnerstan' orders an' jump to it, no argument, no question. An' I'll tell 'em never look in de massa's eyes. Dat gets niggers whipped faster'n anythin'.'

Next day after their morning meal of boiled yams twenty-three children aged from about eight to sixteen squatted round Juliet on the afterdeck. The women were allowed to stand round and watch and, hopefully, learn.

First, they had to be renamed. Most slaves got biblical names, Mary, Samson, Abraham; or classical, like Pompey or Venus. With Bob's help, Juliet tried instead to pick names similar to their own. Hassan became Harry; Gbodi was named Goldie.

Start simply. 'Hand,' Juliet said, lifting her hand. 'Hand.'

Bob repeated it in six languages, 'You say now. "Hand. Hand."'

Hassan lifted his hand. Last night he had decided to set aside his despair. Trying to ignore his seasickness, the hot stench, the low moan of cursing, plans for escape, sobs, complaints, and encouragement in the dark around him, he accepted that he was a slave. It was written thus; he must accept it. So; how could he improve his life? Allah told no man to harm himself by stupidity. In the early dawn he had prayed aloud for the All-Powerful to guard and guide him, and had been surprised and pleased that several voices had been raised to join him. He had repeated the whole first book of the Koran, and felt stronger and more settled. The more he knew, the more he would be worth, and the better he'd be treated. Now, 'Hand,' he repeated clearly.

Silently, the rest glanced at Gbodi.

She hesitated. Omu? 'Learn, to help you fight them.' Yes.

Tentatively she said, 'Han?' and raised a hand. At once everyone joined her, chorusing, 'Han.'

They were going to co-operate! Juliet beamed.

Gbodi beamed right back. This woman—she dressed as a man, but anyone could smell that she was female—she was a fool. Good.

Watching, Dand felt uneasy. The black loon Hassan was fine, a friendly-like skinnymalink, but he didn't trust that wee quine!

He was having his own problems. Against orders, one day Mister Hunt drew a black woman aside, gave her a drink of rum, and was leading her towards his cabin just as Dand came out of Juliet's cabin, where he had been polishing her coat buttons.

If the captain learned of this, he'd be furious. Hunt shoved the girl back towards the door to the deck. 'Out, you demned black bitch! Don't enter here, rot you!' The girl hurried out to be scolded by her friends, leaving Hunt red-faced and fuming.

Within five minutes, Dand and Bert were putting on a show for some of the crew. Dand acted Hunt's embarrassed frustration, while Bert wriggled and giggled nervously like the black girl. The sailors disliked Hunt and loved the joke, but suddenly vanished. Dand and Bert looked up. Mister Hunt was glowering down over the rail above them.

Slyly, Hunt punished the boys. As cook's helper Dand scoured the burnt bits out of the huge pots every evening. Now he was set to help in the hold too. Many slaves were seasick and suffering from dysentery as well, despite the pepper added to their meals. Dand and Bert were always the ones set to empty the stinking latrine barrels, to scrape out the deepest, darkest corners of the hold; they were sent to the masthead, beaten with a rope's end, or deprived of rum for imagined sullen looks. When all else failed, if Hunt saw them doing nothing they were ordered to chip rust off the cannonballs to be sure they would fit neatly into the guns.

Bert just grinned. That was life. They were fine when the captain was around, or under Cartwright's rough but honest glare.

Dand glowered. It was better than being with Maxwell, and far better than Lopez—but some day that rascal would get his dues!

They drifted for ten days of dead calm in the Doldrums, but had enough water. The trade winds recovered before they had to cut the four-litre daily ration.

About a week after that, Dand was skylarking in the rigging with Bert and Hassan. Though not as nimble as them, he could hold a fair place in the races to touch the top of each mast, the far end of the bowsprit and gaff boom, and return to the start. At the top of the foremast, he glanced forward and yelled, 'Ship dead ahead, sir!' He was pleased to have been the first to spot her.

Alerted, the lookout added, 'Plague flag flyin', sir!'

Ahead of Dand in the race, Bert closed horny hands and feet on the rope he was sliding down, braked and climbed back up to swing like a monkey just below Dand. 'Brig *Daisy*, shir!' he shouted.

'No! No!' Dand gasped in sudden furious despair. 'He'll slay me for sure!'

'Not wi' that flag flyin' 'e won't.' Bert slapped Dand's feet. ' 'E's got 'is own worries, mate.'

The *Kestrel* quickly overtook the dirty little brig, which was wandering unsteadily westward under a single flapping sail. Mister Hunt, sent up to the cross-trees with a telescope, reported, 'No one at the wheel, sir. No sign o' life at all. Bodies on deck, sir.'

Captain Owens looked grim. 'Close to hailing distance, Mister Cartwright. Stay upwind of her. Come down, Mister Hunt. Get the blacks below, and bolt down the hatches. We may need all hands.'

The slaves on deck, sensing trouble, muttered and eyed Gbodi. Was this their chance? Omu had no advice for her; she gave no sign. As always, the swivel guns were manned, and blunderbusses ready. Grumbling, the men clambered down, fitting into their places with the smoothness of six weeks' practice, while the women and children were herded back to their cabins.

As the *Kestrel* overhauled the other ship, even upwind her stench caught the throat, heavy and sweet and rotten. Juliet's stomach heaved.

'The bodies are clothed. White men. Dead for some days.' Owens was balancing easily on the bulwarks to see better, a steadying hand on the shrouds. 'No sign of fighting. Perhaps they ran out of water. Or . . . did her captain not say there was yellow fever in Bonny, Mister Cartwright? Whoever gave him the news may have passed on the disease also.' His face was grim. 'Hail her, if you please.'

'Ahoy, *Daisy*! Is anyone aboard?' Six times Cartwright bellowed into the speaking trumpet. The only sound was the creaking and slapping of sails and wood. Even the slaves below were silent.

'No answer, sir,' Cartwright reported unnecessarily. 'Board her, sir?'

'Worth a demned fortune in salvage. To the owner an' us all, sir. Volunteers, sir?' Hunt looked half eager, half afraid. 'I'll go.' Some of the men grinned, while others shook their heads.

'No.' Owens's tone was final. He was aware of how much this would be resented—it could make some of them richer than they had ever dreamed—and chose to explain his reasons. 'I once served on a ship struck by yellow jack. Everyone fell ill. Three quarters of our crew died, as well as most of the slaves. The slave deck was more foul and terrifying than your worst nightmare. Bloated, unrecogniz-able shapes overnight, rats and flies and maggots . . . The stench, the heat—even the hardiest men fell stricken unconscious within minutes while we struggled to haul out the rotting bodies. Those few of us who were able to stand.' Juliet was not the only one to shiver. 'God have mercy on the souls of those who died here, and I appreciate the possible gains, but no, gentlemen, I'll not risk bringing that on board. Nor will we leave her to tempt others to their doom. We shall burn her.'

Hunt glanced at Juliet with a grimace of sympathy. 'I tried, sir. Offered to board. A demned pity, rot me!' he whispered.

Juliet nodded silently; he hoped she would tell her father that Owens had reduced his profits, while Hunt had tried to increase them. Crawling villain! But it had taken courage to offer; she couldn't have done it, in case it had been allowed.

She felt a creeping pity for Hunt. With no rich or influential relatives to help him on, not clever, handsome, or talented, he felt his only hope of promotion was by toadying. This desperate courage was the first admirable thing she had seen in him. Or had he maybe guessed that Owens would refuse, before he dared to offer? Poor little man . . .

A calabash was tied to a line. The cook filled it with hot coals from the stove, and before it could burn through, it was whirled round a sailor's head and hurled into the sag of the *Daisy*'s sail. A whuff of flames mounted the dry canvas, almost invisible in the bright sunlight, marked only by the char that spread, fluttered, and shredded below them.

'Draw off, Mister Cartwright, and assemble the men for church. Dand, bring me my Bible.' While they shuffled into their lines as if for the Sunday sermon the captain took off his hat and began the solemn service for burial at sea. A spar crashed, carrying the fire down to the hull. 'We now commit their bodies to the deep, in sure and certain hope of resurrection to the eternal life to come . . . ' The death ship burst into a final roaring blaze, black smoke rising raggedly to stain the sky. They watched silently until the *Daisy*, and her dead crew, and her six hundred dead slaves, slid hissing under the waves with a final rush of smoky bubbles.

Dand felt relief, and regret. Iain, his friend, would never see Jamaica. Nor the one-legged cook, nor anyone. Even Maxwell's death dismayed him unexpectedly. But as his fear and tension slackened, he found himself grinning. He was free. He felt as if he could fly!

Depressed and distressed by the tragedy, hot and sticky, Juliet went down to her cabin to be alone, and to wash in private. At first, when she withdrew like this, a few eyebrows had been raised, but soon it was accepted; that was the gentry for you—and the owner's son was allowed his odd little ways. No one had even asked why, if she was so eccentric as to want fresh smallclothes more than once a week, she didn't order a seaman to do her wash for her.

'Here ye are, sir!' Dand heaved a wooden bucket of hot water from the galley up to the table for her. 'Just cry on me when ye want it away, eh? Will Ah scrub yer back?'

'Cheeky monkey!' Laughing, she chased him out. She stripped off her belt, her sweaty shirt and binder, and dropped them on the pile of washing by the bucket. Lud, hot water was wonderful! She dipped her cloth in the soap bowl, and rubbed her face—

The cabin door opened. 'Mister Smethwick, have you got—' Hunt stopped. So did her heart.

She had let Dand distract her from bolting the door.

'What the devil? A girl? Rot me.' Slowly, a nasty leer spread over Hunt's face. He stepped in and closed the door behind him. 'God rot me sideways.'

For a moment, Juliet was frozen with shock. The dirty grin on Hunt's face, though, and his rough fingers on her bare arm, snapped her awake. She slid a hand aside, under her shirt . . .

'A demned skirt. Eh? Hidin'. What would the captain say, eh?' Hunt laughed, a low, breathy chortle. 'Or maybe he knows. Maybe he brought you on board, put me out o' me cabin for his demned fancy lass. Old Mister Religious! Who'd 'a' thought it?' He pulled her in towards his wet grin—and stopped at a click and a pressure at his waist.

He looked down. Her pistol was pressed against his stomach, cocked ready to fire.

'You told me to keep it handy, it could save me.' She made herself stand still and smile slightly, though she felt more like pulling the trigger. Or screaming. Or both.

'You wouldn't.' Standing very still, he smirked, not too confidently. 'Shoot me? You couldn't, rot you! No demned trollop could!'

'Couldn't I? I'm not sure myself. But I'm not a trollop, damned or not. Not yours, not the captain's.' She shrugged. 'Why don't you kiss me and we'll find out?'

'You're not with the captain? Rot me if I don't believe you. You'd never have kept it secret.' He drew back, lingeringly letting her arm go, sliding his fingers like slugs over her skin. 'A demned impostor, then. I should tell him. Rot me, it's me absolute duty to report you.' His breath hissed through his teeth. 'Unless you made it worth me while, eh?'

Staring at each other, they both jumped as Dand knocked on the door and half opened it. 'Ready, sir?' he chirped blithely from the passageway. 'Empty yer bucket?'

Hunt's expression was excited and vicious—but in front of a witness he'd do nothing to harm his good fortune. Juliet turned her back and quickly hauled on her shirt. 'I'll see you later, Mister Smethwick.' Hunt stressed the name, gloating, and shoved out past Dand.

She was saved for the moment. He meant to blackmail her. What could she do? She mustn't be found out . . .

Dand had come in and shut the door. Clutching her shirt together she was absently pleased to find her voice quite steady. 'I'm not ready yet—'

'Is that right, sir, that ye're a quine? A lass?' The lad's face was full of admiration, not derision, his eyes almost hidden behind his cheeks in a delighted grin. She found she couldn't answer him. He nodded, as if she had. 'Never fear, sir, naebody else heared. That's why Ah come in. Dod, what a joke, eh? A quine! Good on ye, sir!'

She drew a breath—the first, it seemed, for years. 'You'll not betray me? Thank you, Dand!'

'Ach, it's no' more nor Ah'm due ye!' He sobered. 'But ye'll no' want found out.'

'It would ruin me.' She had thought she had faced the possibility before she began, but the sudden threat of really being discovered, now, after success for so long, was stunning. She would lose everything. Grandmama's shares, respect, everything . . .

Deal with Dand first. She could have the vapours later— oh, mama, she sympathized now! 'I'm Juliet Smethwick, not Anthony.'

'Ye're in the firm? Aye, well. That Hunt—he'll make ye pay for to keep him quiet. Aye.' Solemn now, Dand nodded. 'An' no' in silver, Ah'm thinkin'. That wouldn't satisfy him. Hurtin' folks, he likes that, masterin' 'em. That's why he's a slaver. He'll want to hurt ye. Though what he can do, wi' yer dad the owner, an' no' hurt himsel' . . . He'll think o' somethin'.' He patted her arm to comfort her. She stiffened; he'd not have dreamed of doing so before. 'Never you fret, sir. We'll sort him for ye, me an' Bert. Time he got salt on his tail! You get on an' wash yersel', an' just go on as usual. But mind an' bar yer door, eh? Oh, an' ease yer barker afore ye blow yer foot off!' Winking, he vanished, leaving her speechless.

To her annoyance she felt relief, not insult, that a scruffy brat could feel he was her squire, her protector. But he was a queerly cheering little imp.

Captain Owens had been angry enough when she smuggled Dand aboard. At this deception . . . her stomach shrivelled in dread. If she had been found out within a few days, he would have angrily sent her back in disgrace from Portugal or Madeira. Her friends might never have found out. At worst, they would have giggled and laughed and despised her—but they did so already. Some might have even secretly admired her for her boldness. Her family would have been furious. No decent man would marry her. That was unimportant; it was not her ambition anyway. But now, after months in the company of so many men, alone and unchaperoned, her reputation would be totally ruined. No respectable person would even speak to her. She would be outcast.

She would have to do what she had said, almost as a joke; run away, stay as a man. Could she do that? Really?

Puffing, swearing under her breath, trying to think, she took Dand's advice, uncocked her pistol, bolted the door, and got on with her washing.

During the next watch a heavy block fell from an upper spar, brushing Hunt's shoulder before digging a deep dent in the planking. No one was near it except the boy Bert. White with shock, Hunt cursed the bosun for allowing a rope to get so frayed.

From the deck, Dand exchanged a wry glance with Bert. Ach, well; better luck next time.

When the captain took over the evening watch, an hour later, the carpenter called him away to inspect rot in the forepeak. Cartwright went to his cabin to write reports. The blacks were being fed on deck, excited and twitchy after the morning's events; by the swivel guns the sailors were tense, sensing the atmosphere.

On the after deck, the youngsters assembled for their English lesson. They were speaking a few words among themselves, Juliet noticed with pleasure, using English as a common language for all the tribes. That boy Harry was doing very well—she still felt guilty about how he had been taken, but she couldn't do anything about it, she must just put it sensibly from her mind. Little Goldie was learning fast, too, and David, and—

'Mister Smethwick!' Hunt touched her shoulder. She stiffened, but he was smiling, like a weasel studying a hen. 'You know you have my cabin? To allow the owner's son—' maliciously, he stressed the word slightly '—some privacy. I trust you've appreciated it.'

Conscious of the listening helmsman, she nodded. 'Indeed, sir.' What did he want?

'A rare thing on shipboard, privacy, sir. I share with

Cartwright.' Hunt chuckled. 'He snores—as the whole ship knows! I wondered, sir, if I might beg a small favour? Would you allow me the use o' your cabin for the rest o' this watch, to . . . er . . . relax?'

What? But it could be true. She herself was certainly glad to get away from everyone for a few hours. 'Certainly, sir. Pray give me a moment to tidy it.'

'Ever your debtor, sir, rot me if I ain't.' Beaming in satisfaction, Hunt bowed his thanks, too elaborately.

What was he up to? She ducked along the passage to lock her chest, so that he couldn't steal anything, and returned to the deck. 'The cabin is free, sir!' She sat down on her usual stool with her pupils squatting around her in that flat-footed way she could never copy.

Leisurely, Hunt beckoned to the nearest girl, who happened to be Gbodi. 'Ye'll allow me to borrow her awhile.' It wasn't a question. As the girl rose, smiling as always, he lifted a bottle half out of his coat pocket so that Juliet could see it, smirked and led the girl towards the door to the cabins.

Juliet stiffened again. A girl, and a bottle of rum. To her cabin. Alone.

Even if she noticed, her mother, arrogant and self-centred, would think nothing of it. Her sisters, delicately reared in total ignorance of human nature, would never have understood. But unlike them, Juliet had often visited her old-fashioned, earthy, tough-minded and outspoken grandmother. She knew what Hunt was at—oh yes, she knew.

This was the price for not speaking; her silence, her complicity, over and over, as often as he liked, during the rest of the voyage.

It was against the captain's orders, but on any other ship, it would be normal. Probably it would happen to the girl within a week of reaching America anyway.

If she made any fuss, Hunt would tell. Her secret would be out. What would the captain do?

What did a slave girl matter? A little black savage, half animal . . .

Thy neighbour as thyself . . .

The youngsters of her class, the women gathering behind them, all their eyes were on her. All the dark faces, watching her, waiting to see what she would do. Don't look in their eyes, the big black eyes with the yellow whites . . .

But she couldn't help it. And she knew they were people like her, they felt shame and fear and pain like her, they were as human as she was. They were her neighbours. She couldn't, could not, consent to this, not for herself, and so not for any other girl.

She'd call his bluff; threaten to tell Owens herself. It might work, and if it didn't, she would tell, rot him, she would! She had to live with herself afterwards. Even if it meant discovery, failure, loss of any chance of running the company, total ruin, she couldn't sit silent and ignore it. She might regret acting—jeering at herself, she knew even as she rose that she would regret it—but it was the right thing to do. She'd regret worse not acting.

She jumped down the steps, opened the door—

From the passage came a yelp of outrage.

Behind her the women exploded into riot.

E ver since they came aboard the men had been planning. 'For clubs we can use those sticks the white men tie ropes to—I have a sharp piece of iron—Pull the thorn that sticks out at the side of an iron firestick, it will bark and kill a man—Many of us, few of them, if we all act together we can surprise them, kill them all with our bare hands—Yes, tear them to pieces, like lions!'

Hassan argued, 'Can we swim as far as the ship has travelled? We must leave enough of the white men to make the ship carry us back. The white men have many guns. Certainly many of us will die. Is it worth dying, to be free?'

Someone moaned, 'We'll never be free!'

But others hissed 'Yes!'

'No, no! Dying before you have to is stupid!'

'Stupid?' Hassan cowered at the insulted snarl and slap from a former guard. He was wasting his time, anyway; among the score of tribes aboard, few men would interpret for him, and fewer would listen.

He sensed the sudden tension when Misterhunt took away the heathens' revered holy woman. Even so, it was the men he had expected to riot. The women caught him, literally, off balance. He was jostled along in front of their screaming charge, down the steps and through the door. A big woman behind him misjudged the height of the low door, banged her head and staggered; he had a split second to see ahead.

The young white imam who had been teaching them English spun in terror to face them. By an open door beyond him Misterhunt let Goldie go and turned, pulling a pistol from his belt as he backed off down the passage.

In that instant, Hassan knew what he must do. He grabbed the teacher and yanked him aside through the open door, knocking the black girl ahead of them. The young man tripped. Hassan threw himself on top of him. 'No stand up!' he hissed. 'Sh! Shut you mouth!'

All the breath driven from her, held by her attacker's light but wiry strength, Juliet had little choice for a moment, and as she realized what he was doing and saying she stopped struggling. She wriggled enough to get out her pistol, and then lay still, hidden by his body from the howling women attacking Hunt in the narrow passageway.

Gbodi, shocked and angry, prayed. Omu, what should she do?

On deck, emptying a sack of beans into the cauldrons, Bert had seen what Hunt did. 'Hey, Mishter tally-ho Hunt's huntin' trouble!' he was chuckling to Dand, when Gbodi cried out. At the women's scream of fury, he screeched, 'Climb, Dand! Get high up!' He grabbed Dand's shoulder, shoving him towards the rigging.

The men on deck, warmed from dancing and chanting, took fire from the women. They dived baying towards the white men, clutching, seizing rope, wood, anything that might serve as a weapon. Below Dand a cauldron clanged and rolled. He glanced down between his feet at a squawk and thud, but black hands were reaching for his ankles and he scurried on upwards.

At the crosstrees he stopped. There was no sign of Bert.

Slaves were boiling up from the hold to join the riot on deck. Trapped in a corner, Cartwright and three sailors had fired their pistols and with their long seamen's knives were warding off tearing hands and swinging belaying pins. Luckily for them, the sailors on the raised deck were alert. They fired almost at once, wounding several blacks and holding them back till the mate and the sailors could scramble over the rail to safety.

At the first screams and the bang of a blunderbuss Captain Owens had run up through the forehatch and climbed nimbly across the rigging to the quarterdeck. Now, standing calmly by the wheel, pistol in hand, he had a swivel

151

gun fired over the slaves' heads, as a warning. The tremendous crack brought silence for a second. 'Fire low! Don't kill them! Drive them down!' he shouted. Another blunderbuss wounded four men in the legs. As more shots were fired the unarmed blacks retreated, screaming in pain, yelling in angry fear, leaping down the ladder to the safe dark below. The sailors chased the last men down the ladder with belaying pins, bawling the usual cry to get the blacks back to their shelves, 'Down, get down! Bed down, you black bastards!'

Four minutes and the riot was over.

At the foot of the rigging lay a crumpled little shape, who hadn't won the race that really mattered; the boy Bert, his neck broken. Dand dropped down to kneel by his friend. 'Ye'd have done it if ye hadn't shoved me up first! Damn they black brutes! An' damn Hunt for stirrin' them up!' His grief exploded; he leapt to his feet. 'Ah'll sort the rogue for ye, loon! Never fear!' He dashed towards the steps down to the cabins.

In the little cabin, Hassan, Juliet, and Gbodi heard the women screeching in the passage outside, a shot and a terrified, animal voice shrieking, 'Help! Help!' A roar of men's voices, shots, shouting. Women's voices, howling in triumph. More shots, screams, and Cartwright's bellow, 'Drive them down!' The thud of blows. Men yelling.

As always in sudden emergency nowadays, Gbodi stood motionless, her mind slowed and open to inspiration from her guide. What would Omu want her to do?

Hassan rolled off the young man—and in a flash, somehow, some softness in the face and body told him that this was—could it be? A female? Pretending to be a man?

From the change in the white person's face he—she—knew he knew.

What should he do? Was it as disgraceful for a white woman to show her face as for a True Believer? But he had heard of women warriors. Was this one?

A split-second decision. The young imam had regretted kidnapping Hassan. He was possibly an honourable person.

152

If this was a secret, it would be better to put him—her—in his debt willingly than try to blackmail her—especially at this moment, when she could get him shot so easily. Hassan grinned anxiously. 'I no say!' he whispered. 'No say! I shut mouth!' He rose to help her up.

Just as Juliet reached her knees, a yelling woman charged into the cabin, waving a pistol as a club. Berserk, she saw Juliet's white skin and attacked her.

'No!' Hassan tried to deflect the blow. He screamed as his arm broke, but still tried to protect Juliet. The woman struck again. The pistol butt thudded on his skull, stunning him, and he crumpled to the deck.

'You die now!' Screeching in her own tongue, the woman raised the club again.

Everything went slow for Juliet.

Her pistol was in her hand. Could she fire? Or was Hunt right, was she too weak, too scared?

You do what you have to do. You find the strength.

What if she just wounded the woman? It would make her angry . . .

How much angrier than berserk could anyone get?

The pistol club was swinging towards her head.

Almost of its own will, Juliet's finger squeezed the trigger.

A deafening crack. Her hand jolted with the recoil.

The woman's head was thrown backwards. She stopped, stepped back, fell back against the door-frame, slumped slowly, slowly, smearing blood down the jamb, her arms and legs splaying out on the deck. Her pistol clattered out into the passage.

In the corner Gbodi still froze in the defence she had found best; her mind withdrawn from the danger, clearly no threat, attracting no attention.

Time speeded back to normal. More of them might come in! Panting, Juliet forced herself to her feet, turned the long pistol round to hold it by the hot barrel, wished she had a seaman's knife, this would have to do, hid behind the door poised to strike . . .

Outside, in the passage, light footsteps pattered past, hesitated, went on. Two thuds. A half-heard whimpering stopped.

Heavier steps and a man's voice. 'Mister Smethwick, sir? Are ye there? Dand? D'ye see 'im? God help us if 'e's dead!' The bosun ducked into the room. Juliet just managed not to hit him. 'Ye're safe, then?' He took in the two bodies. 'Well done, sir!'

'No. No, the boy here helped me.' Still shocked to calm and apparent control, Juliet pointed at Hassan. 'He saved me. Protected me from that woman. She hit him, not me. Gave me time to shoot her.' She was safe. Safe . . . The pistol drooped in her hand, and she firmed her grip with an effort. Must make a good impression if she was going to run the firm. 'Is he alive? And Hunt—Mister Hunt?'

'Dead, sir.' Behind the bosun, Dand's voice was grim. 'Right bad, they women.' And what he had done with the pistol he had picked up, that didn't help. But it was a kindness; nobody could live for long, not torn like that— though maybe longer than he'd want to. And if the rogue had babbled in a fever—no, this was best. For everyone. He deserved it, the scoundrel . . . Poor wee Bert . . .

Whistling, the bosun checked Hassan's head. 'Which this 'un's out cold, just a bump.' He patted Juliet's shoulder reassuringly. 'Ye're shook up, sir. Most men is, the first time. Ye gets used to it. Ye done brave, Mister Smethwick, brave, sir.' He noticed Gbodi for the first time, and blinked. 'Fetch the lass out, lads, when ye're up to it. I'll send a man for the lad, an' clear that black bitch away.' He hurried out.

They all stared at the body.

Juliet couldn't move. 'I . . . I killed her. Never thought I'd have to. Be able to. I feel—I killed someone!' She gulped, feeling very sick.

'Just a blackie, sir.' Dand's voice was comforting. 'That don't count.' Not compared to a white man, he thought . . . 'An' she was tryin' to kill you. Ye had to.'

She nodded vaguely. 'You can do what you must . . . You

get used to it, he said. Used to it?' She half-laughed. Never again, please God!

Gbodi moved her eyes, shook her head and sighed, coming to awareness again. Omu had given her no advice; he must mean her to do nothing. Yes. The riot—she remembered it dimly—it had failed—but she had not, for she had not advised it. She stared at the body by her feet. She dimly recalled a bang. Her chief helper, almost her priestess, was dead. Killed by the woman who dressed as a man, laughing there. The idea of justification, of self-defence, never entered Gbodi's head. Her friend was dead, so it was murder. Another thing to avenge. When she could. She began to smile.

Hassan moaned, starting to come round. 'Come on, Hassan, loon! Come an' let the cap'n see to yer arm, eh?' Dand helped him up, groaning, and jerked his head at Juliet. 'You bring the quine, sir? Cap'n Owens'll be callin' for ye.' The four of them made their unsteady way along the passage.

On deck there was little sign of the riot, apart from a few black bodies crumpled by the bulwarks, most of them moaning, and some planks stained red. Two children were crying in a corner, ignored while the sailors cursed, panted, and rubbed bruises, boasted, laughed in the release of tension.

Amazingly cool, the captain was directing the mopping-up while splinting a sailor's wrist. 'Take four men, Mister Cartwright. No pistols—belaying-pins, to knock sense into their thick skulls. Get them all chained safely. Any badly wounded, send up—ah, Mister Smethwick! Lord be praised!' Owens's face lit with relief and pleasure.

'I am unhurt, sir, but—' Juliet winced as she saw the small body by the mast. 'Bert? Oh, not Bert! Poor lad! He so looked forward to being rated able seaman!' She was dully surprised at the bitter satisfaction on Dand's face.

Gbodi had half expected her followers to blame her for the failure of the revolt. However, when she was pushed into

155

the cabin among them, they greeted her with relief and the same respect as usual. 'I told you,' she said quietly. 'Smile, and do as they say. Did I call on you to fight?'

'You cried out,' a woman protested, and was slapped for irreverence.

Gbodi held up a small hand; the squabble stopped instantly. 'That is truth. I did. I was surprised. But I would have endured. It was not time. Not yet. Our time for revenge will come.'

Gradually the ship calmed down.

The slaves were fettered in pairs again, and fewer were allowed on deck at a time. Most of their wounds were cuts and bullet-holes in the legs, but one man had a pistol ball in his chest. The wound went bad; though Captain Owens poured a little heap of gunpowder on the hole and set a match to it to burn away the rot, the man died two days later. One of the women who had attacked Hunt was identified by blood round her mouth. She was flogged and then hanged beside the bodies of the dead man and the woman Juliet had shot. They were left hanging for days while below them the slaves were fed and danced sullenly and unwillingly, under the threat of the lash.

The other slaves thought that Hassan's broken arm came from attacking the whites, not saving one. His life improved. Most of the men were too sick, too weary and beaten into despair, to persecute him anyway.

Dand, ladling out the beans at mealtimes, was helpful and friendly. 'Hey, Harry, how's yer head? More beans, eh? Now ye say, "Thank ye, sir." Aye, fair grand, loon!'

'Thank ye, sir. I say fair grand, eh?'

Hassan fretted about whether the white man—the white woman—would reward him. She eyed him rather nervously during lessons, but did not talk to him specially. Maybe she did not know herself what she planned to do. He would remain calm, show that she could trust him to stay silent, not remind her of the debt she owed him, which would probably do no good anyway. Muslims were servants of

Allah; he would rely on Allah and His Prophet, blessings and peace be on Him, to guide the white female in the right path and get him out of this misery.

For days Juliet moped. She had killed a woman—a woman trying to kill her, but still . . . She had nightmares about it, and about Hunt, and Bert. Was she not responsible for their deaths? If she had not been here at all, or if he had not thought she would cover for him, would Hunt have tried to attack the black girl? She had to face facts. She had given him the chance.

Aware of her distress, Dand did his best to comfort her. 'Never you blame yerself, sir! It was him as done it. A different man'd no' have touched the wee quine. It was his fault, no yours! An' Bert—that was just bad luck.'

But she had to take a share of the blame. She had broken the rules, in coming at all, and also in not calling the captain at once. Like a spark setting fire to a house, her actions—or lack of action—had led to a man's death.

Well. It was done. She couldn't go back; she had to go on. But she'd not get herself into such a situation again.

Her present situation was precarious enough. As well as Dand, that black lad now knew she was a girl. What could she do?

When at last they reached Charleston they had to land the blacks for ten days at the quarantine island outside the port. Mister Jamieson, Murbles and Smethwick's American agent here in Charleston, took a boat out to meet them and inspect their cargo. He was a small, thin man, amazingly grey of coat and skin, amazingly black of wig, amazingly agitated of manner. 'Ye're the first slaver in for weeks, Captain Owens, weeks, an' your nigrahs are prime, prime. As always, sir! The auction will be by the post office as usual. Scarce need to post notices, everyone knows you're here. Over three hundred, that will take three or four days. Yes, indeedy. Usual terms? Bills of exchange?'

'Certainly, sir. Or rice or sugar, tobacco, rum or mahogany to the value.'

'I'll see you ain't cheated. I doubt there's two hundred coined dollars in the town. Damned wars—ruination of honest merchants, ruination! First our fight for freedom from Britain—and what good it's done us I don't know, though don't tell anyone I said so! No indeedy! Then the Spanish, an' now your war against the French. Privateers an' pirates, eighteen ships at least lost in the last month, the maroons out—'

'Maroons, sir?' Juliet blinked. 'Are they deep red?'

Jamieson cackled again. 'Outlaws, young man. Escaped slaves, failed farmers, drunks, buccaneers, Indians, all sorts o' riff-raff skulkin' half-starved in the hills on every island in the Caribbean, raidin' plantations, burnin' an' murderin', freein' slaves! An' our nigrahs help 'em if they get the chance. They'd do the same. That black French rascal on Haiti, burned the whole island! Dreadful brutality, yes indeedy!'

Dreadful brutality. Like hanging and kidnapping . . . and whipping . . . and the speculum oris . . .

Despite the baking heat, Juliet shivered.

The Links Part

LINK EIGHTEEN
August, Charleston

S ome black boatmen and porters tormented arriving
slaves, playing on their ignorance, saying that they
were going to be cooked and eaten, to laugh at their
hysteria and despair. Captain Owens forbade such nasty
tricks which drove some to leap over the side to kill
themselves. For days Bob Bigtooth had been telling the
slaves what to expect.

Even so, when the ship worked her way at last up to
the Charleston anchorage, and the slaves were called up
fifty at a time for their last hose-down and a rub of oil
to make them look shiny and healthy, some hung back
in the familiar darkness. The sailors squashed that nonsense:
'Up, up and out! Get on, ye black bastards! D'ye love
us that much? We're itchin' to see the back o' ye! Up,
up!'

Those with dysentery were packed with straw, tight and
deep, to hide any mess or smell. Then, with some nervous
laughter to hide their tension, they dressed in cheap slave
clothes and clambered down the ladder to the boats below,
most apathetic and resigned or sullen, but some excited and
hopeful.

Gbodi was eager to go. All across the River with One
Bank her stomach had felt uneasy, and she was delighted to
be going back onto dry land. Her dress, a skimpy sack of
pink cotton, was better than anything her village had
owned, softer than monkey-skin against her thighs. Besides,
her smouldering hate drove out fear, but could not entirely
smother her curiosity.

Crowds of men and women watched the slaves climb out
of the boats onto the wooden jetties, and up to the wide,
smooth street. Most of the men were red-faced, clothed
much like the slaves, barefoot in dirty cotton trousers and

shirts and wide, shady straw hats, though some were dressed fine, like king Captenowens.

Black people, too, thronged the shore, staring and shouting. Some were laughing, jeering as the newcomers stared in awe and fear at the fine, tall wooden or brick houses. Others looked solemn and sympathetic. The crowds, the piled goods, the rooting pigs and dogs were much as at home, but to Gbodi's wonder there were large boxes rolling along on rounds of sticks, pulled by horses, oxen, or mules. In some sat white women in big dresses and hats, holding small umbrellas, giggling and fanning themselves just like the people of the town where Omu had been whipped.

At the memory Gbodi frowned; but Omu was with her, in her mind.

One of her followers wailed, 'What will we do?'

'Learn, smile—and fight them!' What else was there to say? Smiling, her eyes glazed, she inspired them with the truth as she saw it. 'Remember our happiness, our contentment, our good health, our good life at home. Plenty of food and oil to make us fat and sleek, always laughter and kindness, safety, freedom. No one hitting us, driving us. The ghost-faces have kidnapped us, hurt us. So we must fight them! But not openly, they are too strong. Smile and obey them, so that they despise you and ignore you. And then hurt them whenever you can. Work slowly, break things, poison them, kill their animals and their children, burn their houses and their crops. Even if you can do only a little, many littles make a lot. Our gods are here also. Never forget. Never forget home, and revenge, and hate! Tell your children and your children's children. Smile, smile, and fight till we are free!'

The woman's sobs faded to sniffles; then she lifted her head and smiled. Her teeth were clenched with grim determination.

The boatloads of slaves were herded along the streets into a wide open space, and then led off in groups of ten or so. Gbodi was in the fifth group on the first day. They were made to run backwards and forwards along the street for the crowd to see them move, and then lined up in front of a big house. Men came over and inspected their teeth and hands, or led them off to a quiet corner to pry more intimately. She smiled.

One by one they were pushed up onto a platform. A man shouted and banged a stick, and people from the crowd called out bids. Then the slaves were shoved down the steps, a rope tied round their necks, and they were led off like goats.

On the verandah of the nearby Royal Hotel, Mr Jamieson and Captain Owens lounged in creaking rattan chairs, watching the auction, ready to answer any questions about the slaves or terms of sale. Fascinated by the differences, by bright sunshine and heat instead of the grey, cold damp of Liverpool, by loose, white cotton clothes instead of dark, heavy wool, by white dust in place of black grime, Juliet sat beside them. And behind her, smart and trimly dressed, smug and sedate, stood Hassan.

Juliet had worried for days about how to reward him for saving her. Captain Owens's advice had been simple. 'Forget it.' He had shaken his head at her surprise. 'It is not easy, Mister Smethwick. Money would be taken from the boy by his buyer, for in law everything a slave has actually belongs to his owner.' Juliet rubbed her nose in dismay. Logical, she supposed, but nasty. 'Freeing him in Charleston or returning him to Africa seems fitting,' Owens continued, 'but would merely leave him to starve, his only hope of survival to surrender himself to slavers again. Keep him as a personal slave, and he will play on the debt, become impertinent and insolent, and you will in the end have to sell him again, which would distress you. No, Mister Smethwick. Forget him. It was no more than his duty, after all.'

Duty—to save his kidnapper? Juliet bit her lip. 'I might ask what he wants—'

'Ask a slave's advice?' he interrupted, shocked. 'Lower yourself to his level? Never!'

163

At last, though, while they were hanging about in quarantine, she decided that she must do something. She drew the boy aside after a lesson. 'Harry, you saved my life. How can I reward you?'

In hope and fear, Hassan's heart beat high enough to choke him. He had been cursing her for forgetting him. Allah, the All-Knowing, the Compassionate, forgive him for not having trusted Him!

He had thought it all out, talking with Dand and the black man who spoke all languages, who knew the ways of white men. He knew what was the best he could hope for. To her astonishment Juliet got a whole plan laid out before her in broken Scots-English. 'Ye fetch me to England, ye teach me how speak good, how read, write. I be man, I go to Africa. I be cabiceer same like Jim. Grand grand cabiceer! I work fair grand. Me dada he cabiceer Farouk. Farouk he big big merchant. Farouk he fetch many grand thing from Timbuktu, Gao, Algiers. I fetch ye many many slave, oil, gold, ah—' He tapped his teeth and gestured a picture of huge ears, trunk, and tusks round his head.

'Ivory,' Juliet supplied. 'From—did you say Timbuktu? It's a real place?'

'Aye. Many many grand slave, all for ye.' He could offer no more. Was it enough?

She felt breathless. Bringing back a witness that Timbuktu existed, that it was not a fable, like Troy—she would be famous! A native factor there, with contacts and agents, for merely the price of a couple of years at school in Liverpool—papa would jump at it. And Tony could never have done it! Even papa must be impressed! 'Yes! Oh, yes! I'll speak to the captain. I'll look after you. Well done, Harry!'

Tentatively, Hassan coughed. 'Hassan. I Hassan, please. No Harry.'

For a moment Juliet bridled; how dared a slave argue? But it was a small point, and she did owe him. 'Very well. Hassan.'

Hassan wanted to weep with joy. He had thought he would be sold, helpless as a dog. However, he controlled himself to bow gravely, as to Farouk. No jumping about, no screaming and shouting; dignity and calm, to impress the heathen woman. You must look worthy of respect to be given it, his father had taught him.

Now, he kept a cool drink ready for his mistress and the captain, as the girls had done for old Taranah at home. His splinted arm was sore, but bearable. His wretched misery and despair were past. Certainly what was written was written, but his future was as secure as any man's. Soon, *inshallah*, he would be a great merchant, esteemed by his uncle Farouk and the other traders, and the white men also. He would become rich and powerful, with a big house and wives and concubines and slaves of his own. And be an imam as well. Praise to Allah, Who knows the needs of every man!

Mister Jamieson congratulated Captain Owens and Juliet. 'Magnificent prices, gentlemen! A charmin' profit! Mister Smethwick—Mister Richard Smethwick—will be delighted!'

An elderly black man bobbed up in front of the rail. 'Letters, Massa Jamieson, sah! Office boy Noah done brung 'em just now from de post office.'

'Hand 'em up then, boy!' Jamieson reached to take the sheaf of envelopes. 'Ship from England came in this mornin', gentlemen—first for two weeks! Starved for news, we are, yes indeedy!' He glanced through them. One or two he handed to Captain Owens, and then one to Juliet.

'Thank you, sir.' Juliet was surprised. Who would be writing to her? Tony? Grandmama? Or—she gritted her teeth—by now papa must know what she had done . . . She broke the seal of the wrapper, read, and sat staring at it in disbelief and shock.

It was not from her father. It was from a lawyer she had never heard of.

Grandmama was dead.

There was a feeling of warmth among the condolences and legal phrases. 'Mrs Sarah Smethwick was our Deeply Respected Client and Friend for over Forty Years. She informed us Fully of her Intentions regarding your Good Self. Before she fell ill she had already Altered her Will, Bequeathing to you all her Shares in the Firm of Murbles and Smethwick, to be Administered by Us as Trustees until your Twenty-first Birthday. She Instructed us to Inform you Immediately on her Death, and to place our Best Endeavours at your Disposal in the case of any Opposition to the Will, which we shall, of course, be Happy to do.'

Oh, poor little grandmama! But she had a good long life, and she had done what she wanted to in the end. To see to it that the firm flourished; that would be the best memorial for her.

Juliet blinked, trying to take it in.

At this very moment she owned more than half of the Company, even if she didn't get full control till she was twenty-one.

Papa would hate it. As grandmama had foreseen, he would try furiously to set aside the will. But with this lawyer's help—and he seemed to be on her side—she would win. And then papa would have to accept it . . . She could convince papa, now, that she'd do a better job if she was trained. Yes.

She should be weeping for grandmama.

No, she shouldn't. The old lady herself would curse her for mawkish lallygagging. Think of the future, not the past . . .

Maybe that idea of staying as a man would be a help? She could come home as a cousin, child of that wild cousin of grandmama's, who had taken Tony's place on this voyage as a dare? If she could persuade papa to keep the secret, Tony and mama and her sisters would do the same— though that depended on what they had told their friends already . . . They could say that 'Juliet' had died at school . . . It would solve so many problems . . . And cause others, of course, but maybe . . .

166

Juliet lost herself in dreams and plans.

Dand helped row the third boatload of slaves ashore, and then slipped away. He wandered idly round for a while, gawping at the grand brick houses along the wide streets, the shop windows, the busy clatter and bustle. Better than Aberdeen, as Iain had said. Even the blacks grinned; you never saw such open smiles at home. And no chance of chilblains.

A hand clutched his ankle and almost tripped him. 'Massa! Massa!' Lying tucked under the boardwalk in front of a shop, a black woman was weakly holding out her long, bony arm. She was naked and starving, ribs jutting under her dusty grey skin.

A neat, sturdy brown-skinned man came out of the store with a sack on his back. He dropped it onto a flat wagon with two mules, tied to the rail, and bent to put something in the woman's hand. Gasping, 'T'ank ya, massa! T'ank ya!' she slithered back out of sight.

'I'd no' leave a sick cat like that,' Dand commented, disgusted. 'Her master's a brute.'

'Ain't got none, suh. She a refuse slave. Nobody buy her, she too old. Dozen, fifteen like her cleared away dead ever' mornin', 'fore they stink out the streets.' The man eyed Dand shrewdly. 'Thee just done come, seekin' work, suh?'

Dand grinned at the queer-like speech. 'Aye, man. Ah can drive horses, plough an' harrow, scythe an' stack hay— anythin' on a farm.'

The man pushed back his broad-brimmed straw hat to scratch his forehead. 'Ain't many farms round the town as'll take on a free man. Most on 'em's worked by their owners, with mebbe a slave or two. But further out, past the big plantations . . . ' He pointed, and offered helpfully, 'Thee'd best take that road, suh, an' go right up to houses to ask fo' work to pay thy way. Ain't many as'll turn thee 'way, less'n thee steals or begs.' He considered. 'Ain't but few Indians left inland, up off the river, most all been took as slaves or

167

druv off. Or killed. Thee could maybe claim a bit o' lan' fo' thyself, far out, without not much hassle.'

'Thank ye, man.' Dand nodded gratefully. This man's skin was an odd reddish brown. 'Are you a slave?' he asked. 'Ye don't look like a nigger, nor speak like none I've heard on the ship nor round here.'

The man grinned as he saw that the boy was merely enquiring, not insulting. 'No, suh, not neither one. Society o' Friends—that's the Quakers, suh—they don' keep no slaves. Ah's a mustee. Mah daddy was black, but ma mammy was a Creek Indian. They both b'longed to Mistah Ball on Limerick Plantation, but Mistah Quentin on Salem Plantation, he done buyed me when Ah was ten year old, an' he set me free an' teached me. Ah is a free hired man, suh,' he declared proudly. 'Ain't many o' us about, but Ah is free. Lo'd bless yo' path, suh.' He returned to his work.

Round the next corner Dand was jostled outside a huge brick building by four men hurrying in. 'My 'pologies, boy,' one grunted. 'In a rush—ma wife tells me Mrs Lagrange sent in two uppity nigra gals to get whipped in the Work House here this mornin'. You heard? Fine sight—shouldn't miss it!' His friends called him on in. Dand considered following, but he had seen whippings, and excitement was urging him on towards his farm.

In the next street he saw the Smethwick quine on a shaded platform outside a big house, watching the sale of the slaves. That was interesting. He wriggled through the packed crowd to talk up to her. He had paid his debt to her—Dod, a wild lass that, eh?—and she'd be happier with him gone. But he should not just slip away.

'Ah come to say fare-thee-weel, Mister Smethwick, sir. Hassan—how's it goin', loon?' Hassan, in the coolest, shadiest corner, bowed with a broad smile.

'Dand?' Blinking, Juliet returned her attention to the hot, noisy, dusty Charleston street, and leaned down across the rail. 'Off to find your farm? You don't want to go back with us, home to Scotland?'

'Na.' He shook his head. 'Iain's big enough to help da. Ma'll have mourned me, an' got on wi' life. There's nowt binds me there.'

She chuckled. 'You've got your voyage across for free, then? Lucky lad!'

'Aye, sir, Ah am that.' He nodded firmly, thinking of the small pearls still safe in his waistband. 'Ah'll work an' save enough to buy tools an' seeds an' a cow, an' then find a place. Even if Ah have to cut it out the wilderness an' fight Indians for it. Ah'll rear cows, Ah don't know nowt about rice nor sugar. Everyone has to eat, eh? An' Ah'll get a few slaves, when Ah can.'

Juliet made a wry face. 'You don't object to slavery, then? When you were nearly a slave yourself?'

Dand shrugged. 'Luck, sir. There's aye masters an' servants.'

At that moment, Gbodi trotted up the steps to the sale platform, beaming. This was the third time she had been sold. At least no one was being branded this time.

The auctioneer asked, 'What's your name?'

The class on the ship had practised this. 'Goldie, massa, t'ank you. Please ta meetcha, massa.' She bobbed a curtsy. Everyone laughed, pleased. Good.

'Good worker, willin', helpful!' the auctioneer praised her. Juliet, Dand, and Hassan watched as the bids rose. At last, the hammer fell. Mr Jamieson beamed as much as Gbodi; thirty-seven pounds was a very good price for a girl child.

A rope was tied round Gbodi's neck, and she was led over to a carriage which held a white man, a white girl a little older than Gbodi, and a brown woman. The girl beamed at the man just as Gbodi had done when her mother gave her her new necklace so long ago, and ordered the brown woman out of the carriage. The woman pointed at the crowd and protested, though still smiling. The girl's hand lashed out like a snake, slapping the woman's face. The woman climbed down and tied Gbodi's rope to the carriage, while the white man spoke, remonstrating gently till the girl smiled dazzlingly, kissed him, and poked the driver with her sunshade to move off.

The brown woman's face was totally blank. As her eyes met Gbodi's, the child's heart sang. Maybe some of the slaves here were happy; maybe most. But others were not. Willingly, not pulling on the rope, she followed the carriage as it edged out of the crowd. After a moment she took the woman's hand comfortingly. Glancing up at her, she smiled, with her mouth only.

The brown woman was eyeing her carefully. Slowly she returned Gbodi's smile.

As the carriage reached the edge of the crowd, Gbodi noticed Juliet. She waved. Curse her. Smile . . . Smile and hate and fight back. Wise, wise Omu! Behind her she had left two masters dead, and one a slave himself. She would see that more followed them. Blood, blood . . . They might chain her, whip her, force her, but they would never beat her. Inside, beneath her cries and cowerings, her heart would never surrender.

Dand clicked his tongue and shook his head in disapproval. 'A bad bargain, that wee quine, even at a shillin'. I'd no' go nearer than ten miles from her. She's mad, eh, Hassan? See her smile? Doesn't touch her eyes. Never. She hates us. No' surprisin', eh?'

Catching his drift, Hassan nodded. 'She look happy, but no happy. She smile, smile, but in here—' he touched over his heart '—she want kill. Slave on ship speak about girl. Know girl. She bad, bad.' He glared after the child. She had made him a slave. 'She want kill. Kill me, kill master. All master.'

The sight of the little girl, rope round her neck, giving her a beaming smile, had started Juliet's heart burning. 'Yes, Goldie isn't the sweet, biddable child she acts. But even so . . . ' Hatred? Hatred enough to kill? Juliet shook her head, trying to dispute the statement. But it was true. Face facts, even if you don't like them; it was true. Again, she saw

170

herself in the child's place. How would she feel? Hatred was the least of it . . .

This was wrong. Vile. At last she admitted it to herself. She had been angry when the carter whipped his fallen horse, so many months ago. This was far, far worse.

She looked at her friends, Dand and Hassan. 'Using slaves on the plantations—that's easy, but there must be a better way.' They stared, perplexed. 'Look at Goldie there. Kidnapped and sold. Tied and dragged along like a dog. Totally, totally in the power of her owner. Look at you and Hassan. People owning people—it's abominably wrong! I don't know what we can do, but there must be something. Maybe hiring the English peasants being forced out by landlords who want to improve their estates. Or the Scots you told me about, Dand.'

'Aye, Ah see what ye're on about,' Dand nodded at last. 'But see, sir. There's an old wife along there wi' no owner. She's free, but she's starvin' to death. An' here's Hassan. He's a slave, but he'll be better off nor my dad when he's done, an' dad's a free farmer. Hassan'll say the same.'

'Is that true?' Juliet asked. 'Hassan? Do you think slavery is a good thing?'

Hassan frowned, trying to understand. 'Ah! Yes, sir. I happy fetch you slave.'

'No, no! Are you happy to be a slave?'

Hassan shrugged. 'No man happy be slave.'

'A right daft notion, that!' Dand chuckled.

'But you'll deal in slaves?' Juliet demanded, bridling at their impertinence.

'See, sir, slavery's the way o' the world. Ye'll no' change it. Ye take what the Lord sends ye, an' do yer best wi' it. Is that no' right, Hassan?'

Frowning, struggling to understand, Hassan nodded. '*Inshallah*. Allah—God—he order all man. He order slave, he order free. What Allah write, He write. Man no can change.'

Juliet snorted. 'Well, I'm going to try! I'll look for other goods, other markets.'

171

Dand grimaced. 'Ye'll no' find none as makes the same profit.'

Juliet hesitated, and then said the ultimate blasphemy— as her father would have seen it. 'Profit isn't everything.'

She looked past Dand's doubtful face to where Captain Owens was laughing with Mr Jamieson. 'He's not a bad man, the captain. He thinks he's a good man, and in many ways he is. But in this he's wrong. Wrong. The slave trade is too terrible, too shameful . . . ' Hassan was frowning, trying to follow her urgency.

What a release it was, to settle at last for what was right! 'You say I can't change things. Well, I'm going to try!' Juliet was suddenly full of energy again, full of vigour and strength, not exhausted by fighting her instincts. 'I'll cut back on slaving in the firm, as hard as I can. I'll work to help change the laws, to stop it.'

'An' ye'll make all the differ, eh?'

'Yes, I will!' she defied Dand's doubt.

The boys looked at her, rather cynically. 'Best o' luck, then. More power to yer elbow.' Half understanding, Hassan smiled and bowed assent. Dand chuckled. 'Ah'll be on my way.'

'Goodbye, then, Dand. And good luck. Thank you for . . . for everything you've done for me . . . ' Including what she suspected but would never know . . .

He grinned, winked, reached over the rail to clasp hands with Hassan—who looked startled, and then bowed, grinning—and vanished through the crowd.

She looked after him, and after Goldie, and then smiled at Hassan. She had a few years to convince him that she was right. He, and Goldie, and Dand, had taught her so much in the short time they had been linked together so unexpectedly. Now she had the chance, and the power, to do something about it.

Those dreary, pious abolitionists in Liverpool were in for as much of a shock as papa, when she got home!

She thought grandmama would be pleased with her.

GLOSSARY

acos	because
anker	small barrel
argy-bargy	argument
aye	[1] yes [2] always
bailie	magistrate
bairn	child
barmy gobbin	fool
barracoon	slave barracks
besom	broom; so, witch, nasty woman, naughty girl
buffleheaded slubberdegullion	fool
cloth-headed dollops	fools
cock-nosed flummery	snobbish nonsense
coffle	group of slaves tied together for a journey
dod	god
doxy	woman of the streets
druv	driven
fetish	holy; object to be worshipped
gab, gob	mouth
gawmless	useless, brainless
ging	go
gowk	fool
hack	deep, painful crack in hard skin, e.g. on feet
Haji	title given to someone who has made a pilgrimage to Mecca
hinny	honey, dear
juju	magic, holy

ken	know
lessen	unless
lingo, linguist	language, translator
long-shanks	tall person
loon, loonie	boy, small boy
lor lumme	Lord love me
luck-penny	penny as a tip
lud	lord, god
mart	market
Martinmas	Saint's day, 11 November
mawkish lallygagging	foolishly sentimental softness
namby-pamby	weak
nincompoop	fool
nobbut	only, nothing/no one but
owt/nowt	anything/nothing
peck	old measure of quantity (2 gallons/9 litres)
prigs	thieves, pick-pockets
pun'	pound
quine	girl
shadoof	weighted beam to dip water out of a pool or river
siller	silver, coins, money
snow	small ship
sozzlin' sots	drunkards
supercargo	officer in charge of a ship's cargo
thon	that, those
top the nob	act arrogantly
uppity	impertinent
vapours, the	hysterics
will we or nill we	whether we want to or not

Further Reading

Travels to discover the Source of the Nile, James Bruce, 1790.

Travels in the Interior Districts of Africa, Mungo Park, 1799.

Journal of an Expedition to Explore the Course and Termination of the Niger, Richard Lander, 1832.

West African Passage, Margery Perham, an internationally-respected authority on colonial administration in Africa; her diary of her travels in Nigeria, Chad, and the Cameroons, 1931–2 (Owen, 1983).

Slave Captain, intro. by Suzanne Schwarz. Journals of James Irving, d. 1791; captured in Morocco 1785 (Bridge Books, 1995).

Transatlantic Slavery—against human dignity, National Museums and Galleries on Merseyside (HMSO, 2nd edn., 1995).

The Slave Trade, Hugh Thomas (Picador, 1997).

The Social Record of Christianity, Joseph McCabe (Watts & Co. (Thinker's Library), 1935).

Slaves in the Family, Edward Ball (Viking, 1998).

Also by Frances Mary Hendry

Chandra

ISBN 0 19 275347 9

'Call me Chandra. My name is Chandra. Remember my name, not just that I am your wife, please.'

Chandra was eleven and she was about to be married to a boy aged sixteen. What could go wrong to spoil her happiness?

But out in the desert she realized she was alone and far from home. She sat in the darkness of her little room, unwilling to accept what had happened to her.

She tried to remember who she was, she hung on to her name. 'My name is Chandra. And I'll not let it be forgotten.'

Other Oxford books

The Breadwinner

Deborah Ellis
ISBN 0 19 275284 7

Afghanistan: Parvana's father is arrested and taken away by the Taliban soldiers. Under Taliban law, women and girls are not allowed to leave the house on their own. Parvana, her mother, and sisters must stay inside. Four days later, the food runs out. They face starvation.

So Parvana must pretend to be a boy to save her family. It is a dangerous plan, but their only chance. In fear, she goes out—and witnesses the horror of avoiding landmines, and the brutality of the Taliban. She suffers beatings and the desperation of trying to survive. But even in despair lies hope . . .

'We've heard and read millions of words about living under the Taliban, yet it remains a distant horror. But . . . [*The Breadwinner*] brings everything to poignant life.'
The Independent

'This beautifully written book is a timely reminder of the courage women and children had to find before the Taliban regime was finally toppled.'
Mail on Sunday

' . . . very remarkable and highly topical novel. The horrors of life under the Taliban are balanced by loyalty, courage and hope. Read it.'
Independent on Sunday

The Dark Ground

Gillian Cross
ISBN 0 19 271925 4

Robert finds himself alone and naked in the middle of thick jungle. He has no idea how he got there. The last thing he remembers is being in an aeroplane on his way back from holiday.

Where is he? Did the plane crash? Are there any other survivors? What has happened to his family?

As Robert struggles to stay alive, he slowly begins to realize that he is not entirely alone. Something—or someone?—is stalking him. Watching him . . .

Who else is in the jungle? Why are they hiding from him? What do they want from him? And how will he ever get home?

Praise for Gillian Cross:

'Cross writes taut, unputdownable thrillers.'

Glasgow Herald

'A superb writer.'

Lindsey Fraser, *The Guardian*

Gold Dust

Winner of the Whitbread Award
Geraldine McCaughrean
ISBN 0 19 275359 2

There's a hole outside the shop. It's just appeared overnight.
And then suddenly there are holes all over town—even in
the main street. The cars can't use the road, everyone has
to walk around balancing on planks of wood, and the whole
town is starting to crumble.

It's started. The secret's out. People are coming from all
over the country. Their hopes are high. The word on
everyone's lips is—GOLD!

'spell-binding from start to finish'
Books for Keeps

'a rich tale of the lust for money that undermines an entire
Brazilian town'
The Guardian

'This novel is pure gold dust'
Times Educational Supplement